About the author:

Marie Cardinal, the distinguished French novelist, was born in Algeria in 1929. She studied philosophy in Paris and has taught at the Universities of Salonika, Lisbon and Montreal. Her first novel, *Écoutez la Mer* (Julliard, 1962) won the Prix International du Premier Roman. Since then she has written twelve other books, including the prize-winning autobiographical novel *Les Mots Pour Le Dire* (Grasset, 1975), published in this country as *The Words To Say It* (The Women's Press, 1993), now an international bestseller. Marie Cardinal has three children, and divides her time between France and Canada.

About the translator:

Karin Montin lives in Montreal where she works as a freelance translator, editor and technical writer. She also teaches translation and is continuing her education in women's studies.

Also by Marie Cardinal from The Women's Press:

The Words To Say It (1993)

MARIE CARDINAL
Devotion and Disorder

TRANSLATED BY KARIN MONTIN

Published in Great Britain by
The Women's Press Ltd, 1991
A member of the Namara Group
34 Great Sutton Street, London EC1V 0DX

First published in France as *Les Grands Désordres* by Editions
Grasset & Fasquelle, 1987

Reprinted 1994

Grateful acknowledgement is made to the following for permission to reprint
copyright material:
The Hogarth Press for extracts from the English translation of J Laplanche
and J B Pontalis, *The Language of Psychoanalysis*, translated by Donald
Nicholson-Smith, The Hogarth Press and the Institute of Psychoanalysis,
1973. The original French edition was published under the title *Vocabulaire de
la Psychanalyse* by Presses Universitaires de France, 1967.
Pantheon Books for an extract from the English translation of Louis de
Broglie, *Physics and Microphysics*, translated by Martin Davidson, Pantheon
Books, Inc, 1955.
While all efforts have been made to trace the holders of copyright, this has
not always been possible. The author and translator would appreciate being
notified of any corrections or additions.

British Library Cataloguing-in-Publication Data
Cardinal, Marie, *1929–*
    Devotion and disorder.
    I. Title   II. Les grands desordres. *English*
    843.914

ISBN 0 7043 4247 2

Typeset in 10/12 Bembo by
Input Typesetting Ltd, London

Printed and bound in Great Britain by
BPCC Paperbacks Ltd
Member of BPCC Ltd

For Alexis, Bénédicte, Benoît, Bruno, Dorian, Frédo, Murielle, Tani, Titi . . .

She was wearing a sober grey suit and black stockings, with a pink and mauve scarf knotted around her neck.

Tall and blonde, in her forties, she moved and spoke the way people do when they enjoy a certain reputation.

A tray with two cups and a plate of biscuits had been prepared in my honour. She asked me to sit down and left for what must have been the kitchen, saying, 'I'll get the tea. Will you have some or would you prefer coffee? Juice? Anything else?'

'Tea would be fine.'

The living room was pleasant, done up in the 'colonial' style: potted trees, curtains of Indian cotton, white goatskins on the floor. I noticed that I was sitting in the only armchair. Apart from that, there were cushions and a red leather sofa, somewhat worn but still handsome. Everything was a little dilapidated; the cups and saucers didn't match. On the wall hung paintings and prints that I would later look at and love, but which at the time just attracted my eye.

She returned with the teapot, poured a cup, handed it to me, and poured one for herself. 'Help yourself,' she said, pointing to the biscuits. She sat on a cushion. I could see that she was used to sitting on the floor. She had a precise way of gathering cushions around her and arranging them to make herself comfortable. I was surprised. I had been expecting to meet someone more conventional. All at once I was the one who felt conventional, sitting in my armchair. She intimidated me.

She began to talk.

'As I mentioned on the phone, Dr Bourget is the one who put me in touch with you. I thought his book on nutrition was very good, far superior to most. Nowadays, books on nutrition . . . you know what I mean. But his is fascinating: it's well written, it makes you think and it's a pleasure to read. I met Dr Bourget and congratulated him on it. He's the one who told me how you'd helped him write his book and gave me your number. Have you been in this line of work for long?'

'Ten or twelve years – no, actually more like fifteen.'

'How does someone get started writing other people's books, if I'm not being indiscreet?'

'Not at all. At first I did it to earn a living, and now I do it because I like it. It's still writing, and I learn all sorts of new words from different fields. It allows me to write my own books.'

'Oh, I'm sorry, but I haven't read any of your books. What do you write?'

'Novels, mystery novels, actually. At least, my aim is to write novels that critics won't simply call mysteries.'

'And don't you manage to?'

'Yes, I do, but they aren't very popular. They're thrillers, in a way – but not exactly. It's an unknown genre in France. Here you have to be able to slot books neatly into drawers with labels. I don't make a living from them.'

'By the way, I don't know your terms.'

'It depends on the job. I usually ask for a lump sum, and if I have to spend a lot of time and energy, I also ask for a percentage of sales.'

'As a ghostwriter – that is the right word?'

'Yes, that's right.'

'Do you chiefly do nonfiction?'

'Almost exclusively. But let's get something straight: I don't write, I translate. I try to get under the skin of the person whose name will be on the cover, to identify with the person. I use everything I'm given, everything I see and hear: words, photographs, writing, verbal tics . . . I'm part chameleon; I like doing it.'

'I can see you enjoy your work. You know, it's funny, but I did the same kind of thing a long time ago, when I was a student. So that I could bring up my daughter and go on studying, I worked as a secretary for Professor Greffier. You've probably heard of him; he nearly won a Nobel prize a few years ago. He's a physicist, a specialist in thermo-dynamics. He had me correct and type up popular science articles he wrote for magazines. Oh well, it's not really any-thing like what you do; I never wrote anything myself, I just corrected his grammar and spelling. I learnt a lot. But that's ancient history.'

She began to talk about what she liked to read and what she had read. In passing, she gave me an unexpected pleasure: she mentioned Chester Himes. In her opinion, if you wanted to understand New York, you had to read his crime novels. To return the courtesy, I told her he was one of my idols, which is actually true.

She had a beautiful deep voice, and she used it to charm. We were having one of those polite, refined conversations. A mature, still attractive woman was talking to me about literature. In my opinion she didn't know a great deal about it. I wondered what I was doing there.

She could tell that the conversation didn't interest me much. She stopped talking. The silence continued, becoming awkward. I didn't know how to break it. She began to talk again. Her voice had changed; I was surprised how hoarse it had become. It was as if her throat were struggling to get the words into her mouth, and her lips felt them, becoming aware of their shape and meaning before letting them out. At first I thought she was putting it on, but then I saw that she was very moved. She intrigued me and I listened attentively.

'I need to write . . . I think I need to write. I have been through a rather . . . unusual . . . experience. I feel it's my duty to share it. Perhaps other people might benefit from it. Perhaps, too, I need to free myself from it . . . I don't honestly know what I want. I'm a little bit lost. I've tried to write about it myself, but I'm used to the academic style of scientific and theoretical papers and textbooks. That's not the kind of writing for what I want to express. I've lost the touch. I can't avoid the royal we that "scholars" use . . .'

She raised a finger on either side of her head to indicate the quotation marks around *scholars*, at the same time making a dunce's cap. She smiled.

'The first person singular is too private; it seems indecent to me, somehow. And yet it is about me; I want to relate something that happened to me personally. I played with *I, we, she*, and I didn't get anywhere. I couldn't establish the proper distance. That's why I called you.'

She had got hold of herself; she had regained her self-control. She outlined her story briefly. She had confronted something that I had actually been thinking about for some time.

'Would you be interested in writing about it?'

'I think so, but as I said before, I won't be writing, I'll be translating what you say.'

'All right, then. We'll give it a try. How should we do it?'

'You can tape what you have to say yourself, and I can go over the tapes at home. Or I can come here, you can tell me the story, and I'll record it and take notes. It's up to you.'

'What do you prefer?'

'I'm used to both methods. I don't mind one way or the other. The important thing is for you to feel comfortable speaking and to give me as much material as possible to work with.'

'I'd rather you came here. Hearing my voice, alone . . . hearing myself tell the whole thing, alone, out loud . . . I don't know if I'd have the courage. It would be more natural if you were there. And will you show me what you've done as we go along?'

'No, not as we go along, only when I have a good-sized chunk.'

We agreed to meet twice a week.

Two months later I had a hundred and forty-three pages. I had written most of them myself, but some were straight transcriptions of the tapes. I gave them to her on a Friday; it was 12 December 1979. We were to see each other the following Monday.

I was already a changed man.

PART ONE
The One Hundred and Forty-Three Pages

The First Day

The plane came to a standstill. The clicking of seat-belts could be heard immediately as the passengers escaped, unwilling to remain seated another second: they had been buckled in for close to seven hours, and they had had enough.

Elsa Labbé stood up along with the others. But she was near the window and the overhead baggage compartment prevented her from straightening up. Still she managed to put on her shoes, which wasn't easy because her feet had swollen. She wished she were already at home. Her holiday had been wonderful, but now she wanted to get back to her flat and her research.

As she slowly moved ahead in the line to show her passport, she flexed her thigh muscles; they were fine. She had run, rowed, swum, climbed, and everything had been fine. Each year before setting off she told herself she wouldn't be able to do it this time, that she was growing old, and then after a few days it all came back. The fatigue disappeared. She forgot. She was far from her patients, the telephone, the lack of sleep.

For the last three years she had been spending her holidays with François on the east coast of the United States. She enjoyed getting together with him there, but after six weeks she was happy to leave. She felt as if she had replenished her store of health and nonchalance with him, yet towards the end of her stay she started to miss her work.

And especially Laure.

Leaving the airport, Elsa thought how good life was.

The taxi. The highway. Paris. Except for minor details here and there, nothing had changed. The road had been resurfaced at the Pasteur intersection. The shopkeepers had opened up again. Just before arriving home, she saw the baker behind her cash register. She looked forward to seeing her later, her and her bloody bread.

As she turned the key in her front door, she imagined her bathroom: the tub, the mirrors, the earthenware tiles, the pale furniture, the wicker armchair. She also imagined her bedroom with its double bed, the pink lamp on the bedside table, the bevelled octagonal mirror in its old worm-eaten frame, and she enjoyed the thought. The bath would be warm, the sheets soft, and she would fall asleep listening to the sounds from outside, the sounds of active Europe, although for one false night her body would follow the rhythm of North America again. She liked the uncertainty created by the time difference, the cellular memory that meant the present was elsewhere and that elsewhere was present; she liked the feeling of being everywhere at once, liked it and yet mistrusted it. She mistrusted the appeal of what was suspect, hidden.

Elsa Labbé was a hard-working woman, a reasonable woman, and yet she was drawn to the unreasonable. She knew that she was ambiguous, equivocal, capable of doing anything – that this was one of her basic traits. But because of the way her life had unfolded, she had chosen convention. Or to be more specific, she had managed to make her 'curious nature' conform to convention.

When she was a child, her father used to say, in his southern way, that she had a *'curi-euse nature.'*

And her mother would correct him each time, saying, *'nature curi-euse.'*

'Right,' he would answer. 'Let's just say she's whimsical.'

In any case, Elsa had grown up to be a respectable woman. And until that morning as she looked for her keys in the bottom of her handbag, she had controlled her 'whims' and had not let them lead her astray.

The door opened, and in a fraction of a second Elsa's entire existence was shaken; she didn't understand, she was flung into uncertainty. She stepped forward, set down her suitcase, and closed the door behind her, leaning against it. Her heart was in her throat, choking her. It was a brutal shock; she hadn't been expecting it. She had no time to muster her defences; she was losing her footing. She refused to see what she was seeing, but knew that closing her eyes would do no good. She felt repulsed, revolted: 'Why am I being forced to look at this sight?' And at the same time she felt her old curiosity gaining the upper hand: 'What's going on?'

The thought that her flat had been burgled passed through her mind but didn't stay. She knew that wasn't the answer. What then? What had happened? Was it still happening? She didn't dare move, she was vigilant – watching and listening.

But there wasn't a sound to be heard.

She was standing in the hall. She caught a glimpse of part of the living room, a bit of the kitchen, and the end of the passageway that led to the other rooms. The walls were in their usual places, but they enclosed a foreign, even hostile space, although everything in it was familiar.

The blinds had been lowered and in the half-light the contents of her flat formed indistinct mounds. The curtains had been torn down; some were still hanging by a single ring, like sails on a shipwreck. The furniture was heaped up in places – especially in front of the windows – and was covered with clothes, papers, objects of all sorts. The rug was littered with rubbish and filth.

The whole place reeked.

She was assailed by the stink more than by the ransacking. It stank of abandonment, rape, suicide. It stank of unhappiness; it was unbearable. The smell was alive, but everything else was dead.

As she became accustomed to the dark, she noticed that the drawstrings of the curtains had been arranged to form a kind of spider's web. She tried to work out what the arrangement meant but it was beyond her. She saw that the strings were tied to fishing rods. She recognised the fishing tackle that had been at the back of a store-room full of trunks and other paraphernalia she rarely used, old things she could never bring herself to throw out. Everything would have had to have been taken out of the store-room to find this stuff! Thoughts raced through her mind, colliding with one another. It was beyond belief!

She recalled the holidays when her daughter had been small. Laure had been so serious, with a fishing rod four times her height. She felt a pang in her heart at the recollection, since she guessed – was quite certain, even – that all this had something to do with her daughter. She began to shiver. She wanted to moan but couldn't.

She couldn't moan, she couldn't move, she couldn't do a thing. She was still standing inside the front door, paralysed, stricken by what she had seen, by the sickening smell, by the mess. Motionless anguish, morbid energy were lurking there. The fishing rods . . . and now the nylon lines, coiled from having been left wrapped around their reels for so many years, were advancing towards her, towards the front door. And there at her feet, everywhere around her, were fish-hooks. Small, sharp, wicked, glinting hooks! Tiny Laure again, her blonde hair, honey-coloured skin, boyish body. Bold Laure, arguing, head-strong, going off to fish from the rocks. Off to adventure. 'Careful – don't hurt yourself on the hooks!' The little girl shrugged her shoulders. She hated being treated like a child. She knew she could hurt herself on a hook; there was no point in repeating it.

But what was the matter? What was happening to her? Elsa lowered her head and slid down the door to the floor. She crouched and wept, or rather, tears ran down her cheeks. She didn't sob, and her expression wasn't sad. It was only water, fluid spilling out of her, an overflow. As if she were giving way.

Her child, her daughter, her darling. She had called her several times while she had been away. The first time, Laure had complained that it was stifling in her flat and that she was going to live at Elsa's place where it was roomy and she could create a draught. That had been good news. Laure had the keys; it was only natural that she should use the empty flat. And then, the day before yesterday – although the line was good – she had sounded odd, her voice had been sort of thick and morose. Laure had said she would be going back to her flat that same day.

'Stay there, so I can see you when I get in.'

'No, I'd rather go home.'

'All right, if you'd rather. What's the matter? Are you ill?'

'Of course not! Why?'

'I don't know. Something in your voice . . .'

Now Elsa came to a realisation she had managed to keep at bay for two days: a vague warning that had been sounding since she had returned from the Sydney conference crystallised now around Laure because of that conversation.

Afterwards, in Manhattan, as she and François were crossing an intersection, they had seen a couple: a man and a very young woman, who looked ill; the man had been practically carrying her. Elsa had thought that the young woman looked like Laure. She had stopped to watch the couple walk away. She had felt nauseated. Later she had refused to eat, and François had irritated her. But she had pulled herself together: after all, there had been nothing unusual about the couple, nothing strange about the telephone call. Except Laure's voice . . .

'What's that, Elsa?'

She hadn't wanted to wear black to go to claim Jacques's body, and she had taken Laure with her. Why had she taken Laure? Sometimes she reproached herself for it, but at other times she understood.

Twenty-two and two, that's how old they had been.

Two and twenty-two. A little tiny girl and a very young woman who had gone to fetch the coffin of a man killed at war – alone, without fear, without mourning. As if youth and a military death erased death itself. As if a dead soldier couldn't be a dead father or a dead lover – only an historical corpse for which you were responsible. As if neither war nor history could be an obstacle to girls their age, only accidents along the way.

There had been the sounds of soldiers, orders, the clicking of heels. No music: the repatriation of soldiers killed in Algeria had all been very discreet.

Little Laure, fascinated by the cranes, the bustle of the

port, the boats, the sirens, and the seagulls' cries, had beamed at the officer who had come to shake their hands. As he presented them with a military decoration, he had uttered incomprehensible condolences.

'What's that, Elsa?'

'Nothing, dear. It's just the port.'

Elsa had not answered Laure's question. She had felt incapable of explaining to her all that was going on – death, war, her father, the nation, love, the family, everything . . .

Standing before Jacques's flag-draped coffin, she had first found the situation incongruous: Jacques had hated the army, war, that particular war. Then, precisely because of the absurdity of his death – the lack of pomp perhaps, and Laure's look of wonder at the medal, especially – she was convinced that she hadn't behaved respectably. Something began to disturb her deeply, and she felt she deserved to be punished – yes, punished. She should never have brought the child, she shouldn't have let her see all of this, she should have answered her question, she should have worn black, she should never have let Laure call her Elsa – and one day she would be punished for all of it. That's how she had felt.

She raised her head and started to think again that she should never have taken Laure with her. What had it all done to the child's mind – the long row of coffins, the invisible dead, the flags, the sobbing women, the stuffy men, all that in the midst of the exciting smell of the port, beside a huge ship with a gaping belly? What had it done? She and Laure had talked about it on a number of occasions. Each time, Laure had claimed that she had only a vague recollection, that it was rather a happy memory, that maybe that was why she liked the sea and travelling, that she wasn't even sure whether she really remembered it or just remembered having been told about it.

Suddenly it occurred to Elsa that Laure might still be sleeping in the flat, that she hadn't gone back to her own place. She stood up and called her daughter: 'Laure, Laure!' She walked towards the bedrooms, calling 'Laure' again. But nothing stirred.

Now that she had begun to walk around the flat, she discovered more chaos, more devastation, more disorder with every step. She knew something about disorder, that was her field – she knew the reasonable end of it, the clinical end. But the disorder that she was seeing was not on the road to a cure, not even looking for a cure, and although she had always suspected it must be like this, it was something she had never experienced – only sensed. Insanity in the raw. An explosion of insanity at home, in her flat, frozen there. A couple of slaps in the face, an earthquake, a fire – stuck there, paralysed. She had always been afraid of madness. Perhaps that was why she had chosen her profession: Elsa was a psychologist.

Despite the darkness and the chaotic mess, she could make out papers, a great quantity of papers, mixed up with everything else. That was what shocked her the most, because they were her papers; she recognised them. They were her notes, her charts, her calculations, her research findings, her files, and children's drawings, too, dozens of children's drawings, hundreds of children's drawings, doodles, each one annotated, dated, numbered. Years and years of her life. Her past and her future. Her office had been turned upside down! Her life had been turned upside down! Why?

The smell! Elsa was suffocating.

She turned on the light, opened the doors and windows. Everywhere there was nothing but meaningless heaps. Dirty clothes, dried and rotten food, overturned bottles . . . Everything was in such a jumble that she no longer knew whether there were still beds, chairs, or tables in the rooms. The cupboards and wardrobes were open and empty. Their emptiness added to the senseless chaos.

And that strange, repulsive smell, with its reek of sweat, fermentation, rot, and something else she couldn't identify – something sickly and musty.

Someone had vomited in the bathroom sink. Dried splatters covered the mirror above it. Elsa turned around in the middle of the room; on the white earthenware tiles, between the sink and the bathtub, she noticed several lines of black droplets, dense dried trickles. She stiffened, rejecting images

11

of hospitals, and the word *blood* ran through her mind. She fled from it, wanting to flee from herself, from her emotion. She had to keep a grip on herself. She had to act. In the disgusting mirror she had just seen the reflection of her white coat, the one she wore to receive her patients, hanging in its usual place on a hook on the back of the door. It was the only normal thing she had seen so far.

She undressed and put on her white coat; she was going to clean up.

Retracing her footsteps she no longer looked closely at the devastation. Her mood had changed when she had put on her work coat. First off she would call Laure and give her a good talking to, a talking to such as she had never given anyone before in her life. Who could ever imagine a house so filthy! Who had she let in? How could she have allowed them to do this?

The telephone wasn't working; there was no dialling tone. Out of order. In this neighbourhood things were constantly being torn down and built up, and the phone was always out of order. Before going on holiday Elsa had left Laure some blank cheques to pay the telephone and electricity bills, along with the rent. For the last three years she had been telling herself that she should let the bank take care of all that, but she still didn't have the habits of the well-to-do. But there was no use thinking about that; she had other things to think about. She reassured herself: Everything's fine. The phone is just out of order, that's all.

In the kitchen, stacked haphazardly, were all the dishes, dirty to the last one. All the plates were dirty: dinner plates, soup plates, big ones, small ones; every single serving dish was dirty; all the glasses were dirty, including the crystal goblets that were never used; every saucepan was dirty; every frying pan, every soup pot; everything. There was a container of spaghetti and tomato sauce covered with mould, and on the floor in front of the stove a piece of stinking, rotting meat was abuzz with flies.

She raised the blind. In here the sunlight was even crueller than in the rest of the flat – the walls and ceiling were spattered with disgusting filth, and here too vomit had spilled out of the sink and dried on the doors of the cupboard below.

So, the dishwasher had broken and they had evidently preferred to do nothing rather than wash any dishes or try to repair it. She opened the machine; it was empty. She pressed the buttons; it worked. The dishwasher worked. What then was the explanation? Where was Laure? What had happened while she was away?

She needed to know; Laure had to explain; she must speak to her. She would call her from the phone box on the square at the corner. Elsa went out as she was, in her white coat. She dialled the number and let it ring twelve times. She counted the rings: twelve. No answer. She went back home, returning to her filthy nest. The flat, or rather, the state it was in, had suddenly become her sole preoccupation, her entire life. She no longer paid attention to anything else: passers-by, shops, the normal pace of the people around her. She looked down. Her head hanging, furious, she returned home. They'd soon see! Just wait until she got hold of them! They wouldn't get off lightly! She'd give them a piece of her mind!

But who were they? There must have been a gang of them: even if Laure hadn't washed a single dish in six weeks, she could never have dirtied this many. Elsa set to work scouring fiercely, but the tidier she made the kitchen, the more worried she became. The disorder was positively unhealthy! The spoons were bent, every last one of them. She remembered that as a teenager, Laure had used spoons to take the tyres off her bike, and later her moped. How many tyres had they repaired? She asked the question to reassure herself, because deep down she knew that was not how the spoons had been used. What had they been used for? What game? What rite? Elsa did everything she could to calm down. In talking to herself, she even took refuge in her professional jargon, using a technical vocabulary that suppressed emotion and made sense out of insanity. Cleaning all the while, she analysed the situation clinically and found a word that summarised everything, explained everything: catharsis. Yes, that was it, she was dealing with the devastating consequences of a cathartic event, a crisis of collective folly provoked by some unknown scene – perhaps not a tragedy, or even a drama – a scene that had purged them of their violence, their pent-up taboos. Everything had come out at once. They had vomited their hates and nightmares. They had reverted to savagery.

It was easy to think, but it didn't help her accept what she saw. It didn't dispel her fear; on the contrary, for normally she employed this vocabulary only with colleagues, to communicate with them more quickly.

Catharsis or not, her throat was still so tight that she felt as if she would choke, and still she wondered constantly: What has happened to Laure? On the phone the day before yesterday Laure had said nothing about what had happened in the flat, even though it must have been going on for some time. Elsa knew enough about housekeeping, about food, about decay to know that the filth wasn't all new, that there was filth both old and new everywhere.

'I couldn't care less about catharsis. I want to know what happened and where my daughter has got to.'

Six times that day she interrupted her work to try to get in touch with Laure. Six times she found herself back at the square, enclosed in one of the shiny new transparent telephone booths.

It was late summer in Paris. Despite a nip in the air, she still saw men in shirt-sleeves and women wearing sandals. The umbrellas were even up outside the café across the square – three umbrellas with TUBORG written on slices of white canvas alternating with blue: TUBORG, blue, TUBOR, blue, TUB, blue, TUBORG, blue.

'Even if I read TUBORG a million times I won't be any further ahead!'

There was no answer at Laure's. Where was she? Was she still alive? She thought once more of the young woman in the Manhattan crowd, amidst the Manhattan grime, bracketed by the towering Manhattan skyscrapers, the young woman who had looked like Laure and had been so sick. François had said, 'She's a . . .' What had he said? What was the word he'd used? She was a . . . what?

That morning in the kitchen, she had discovered the first thingummy, the first contraption, which she had wanted to think was an eye-dropper. It was a small plastic device with a plunger. She could have thrown it away, but she had kept it, stuffing it quickly into the pocket of her white coat without really looking at it. The word *syringe* had flitted through her mind, buzzed like a fly at a closed window. She had chased it out, as earlier, in the bathroom, she had chased out the word *blood*.

After the kitchen, she started on the sitting room, and then the other rooms: the office, the waiting room that doubled as a guest room, Laure's old room that was now the secretary's office, her bedroom. She pushed the furniture, putting it back in place, tried to sort through the papers and put her files back in order, piled up the dirty laundry: shirts, trousers, T-shirts, underpants she'd never seen before, in bad shape, all the same style, of the 'I love NY', 'Che Guevara', 'Fruit of the Loom' variety.

'She must have let in a pack of ruffians, a wild motorcycle gang, a bunch of peace and love types still carrying around their parents' abortive dreams of May '68, sinister hippies, misfits, dropouts . . . They've wrought havoc, just for kicks, to exact God knows what vengeance, to settle God knows what accounts, to purge themselves of a past too heavy for them to bear.'

Each time that anger and fear threatened to overwhelm her, Elsa returned to the catharsis theory, because she knew that she couldn't run away from what she was going through, that she couldn't avoid it.

In the passageway, buried beneath blood-stained sheets – 'There must have been some girls in the bunch' – she came upon the telephone bill, unopened; it had been mailed three days after she left. The phone was cut off, that was all, not out of order, cut off because Laure hadn't paid the bill. It was too late for Elsa to do anything about it now; the post office was shut. She would see to it tomorrow. Had Laure taken leave of her senses?

Here and there throughout the flat she found more little contraptions, the things she called eye-droppers, accumulating them in her pocket. They were syringes! Elsa couldn't keep fooling herself. She'd always known they were syringes; she had seen enough of them at the hospital. They were disposable plastic syringes. Some of them even had needles. Eye-droppers – really!

It was ten in the evening and she hadn't stopped. She sat down on the floor in the hall, feeling her pulse throb throughout her body. 'There were all kinds of drug addicts here . . .' Was Laure a drug addict?

When Laure was a teenager, she had wanted to study medicine. She had always been concerned with bodies, her own and other people's. Had she wanted to help the drug addicts and been overwhelmed by it all? In that case, why was she avoiding a confrontation? It wasn't like her; Laure was good at arguing and loved to talk things over. When she pleaded what she thought was a just cause, she was capable of anything, even of being unjust. Why didn't she go to law school? Why did she insist on studying filmmaking?

Elsa kept going back over it all: medicine, law, film. Perhaps they'd used the flat to shoot a film. She'd met the young people her daughter had been trying to make shorts with. They were mad about film, light, lenses. They had seen virtually every film ever made; they spent their lives in cheap neighbourhood cinemas; they knew all the tricks for sneaking in or being let in on the house. They were muddle-headed, passionate, shameless, insolent. Elsa liked them a lot. She didn't think them capable of such devastation.

By midnight she was still far from finished, but the flat was beginning to look more like home; it was less frightening. She had been cleaning and tidying for fourteen hours, and she couldn't go on. She decided that enough was enough, and that she would lie down.

Her bedroom was the least devastated room in the flat. From various small details, Else could tell that Laure had been staying in it. There were Laure's butts in the ashtray – she had the odd habit of smoking each cigarette only halfway; there was the way she draped a scarf over the lamp to subdue the light, and there was a certain scent everywhere: the smell of Laure. Elsa had aired the room, changed the sheets, vacuumed – but still the scent remained.

16

She was lying on the bed, eyes closed. It was midnight at home. Over on the other side of the ocean it was six o'clock, not yet evening. Between her and François was a distance much greater than the six thousand kilometres and the six-hour time difference. The image of François came to her as she lay down because the last time she had been in a bed it had been with him, but she hadn't thought about him all day. What had happened to her since the morning had changed her to the point where anything other than the flat, other than what she had seen and guessed had happened there, did not interest her in the least. She didn't know why she felt so cut off from the rest of the world. She was no longer connected to anything but this city, this evening, and then only by the tiniest of links, incandescent filaments that burnt into her flesh, and at the other end of which was Laure. Laure was in Paris, but where? Where was Laure? Was Laure alive? Where was Laure's body living? She kept asking herself this question, which caused a pain in her stomach and chest – sharp unbearable nips, jabs! Once again she saw the fish hooks in the entrance that morning, glinting, wicked. Once again she saw the trickles of blood in the bathroom; there had been some in the kitchen, too, as well as . . . The pain inside her was fierce. She was floating. She was suspended in reeking air, and a thousand fish hooks were holding her in equilibrium. The least effort to think increased her suffering. How could she think properly? How could she stop the flood of suppositions, doubts, hopes that constantly harassed her? How could she persuade herself that vomit, blood, vandalism, syringes were just that – vomit, blood, vandalism, syringes, and nothing more? How could she persuade herself of that? How could she stop the panic?

Had she been able, she would have continued to wash, erase, obliterate, but she was exhausted, so tired that her body trembled from head to toe, and she was shivering.

No, Elsa wasn't mistaken. In the distance, at the far end of the flat, she had heard the key in the lock, then the front door closing softly. Now footsteps – Laure's footsteps! She couldn't be mistaken; no one else walked the way her daughter did.

She was there. Finally her little girl, her loved one was there!

There at last, framed in the doorway. Thin, alive, beautiful – so beautiful! Elsa was always overwhelmed by how beautiful her daughter was. Laure's pupils were brighter than she'd ever seen them before and a new pallor with dark circles under her eyes disturbed Elsa even more. No more fish hooks, no more torturing herself: Laure was there, on her own two feet. Her own Laure, her beloved!

Their eyes had scarcely met, full of love, full of joy and the eagerness to see each other again. A mother and daughter, as alike as Russian dolls. They had scarcely caught sight of each other, scarcely caught the scent of each other, when their love became instantly obvious. In that fleeting silent moment their most precious possessions, their secrets, rose to the surface . . . The almost imperceptible sparkle in their eyes was all that was needed for their differences and similarities to spring up and mingle so intimately that they became one, they became a torrent, a mountain, a single life beating strong – their life together, robust, simple.

Laure approached Elsa. There was something tragic in the way she travelled even that brief distance from the door where she had been standing to the bed where her mother lay. Everything about her movement was tragic, yet Laure was subdued; it was just this self-restraint, the lack of expression on her face, the slowness of her steps, that revealed her inner turmoil. Elsa felt that her daughter was calling for help. She moved over on the bed to make room for Laure, who lay down with her, almost upon her. Laure's head nestled in the hollow of Elsa's neck, her small hard breasts pressed against her mother's. She sobbed, cried like a baby. She was very distressed and could finally express it. Through her sobs she offered to share with Elsa the thing that was overwhelming her. Her mother accepted without even knowing just what she was accepting; she wrapped her arms around her daughter and rocked her. She, too, felt like crying. She forgot the lecture she had been intending to give her. All she said was, 'There, there. It's all right. The house is in a shocking state, but . . .'

Laure butted her with her head, like a kid. She wanted her mother to be quiet, she wanted her mother to join her where she, Laure, was: 'That's not it! That's not it! I don't give a damn about the house! Listen, Elsa, listen: I'm a druggie. I'm a user. I've got to stop. Help me, Elsa!'

That was all Laure said, but it was enough to push Elsa over the brink and down into the abyss which had been deepening all day, although she had managed to remain on the edge of it so far. It was a frightening fall, an interminable fall that fragmented her existence and scattered the pieces. Nothing held together any more. Elsa was mute, deaf, blind, ignorant – so ignorant! She clutched her daughter tightly. Laure grabbed her, shook her, repeated several times as if it were an order: 'Help me!'

Elsa thought she had fainted, that she was lost. It went on and on. She had even lost her voice. She groped for it. Where had her words gone? She had to speak. She struggled in her stupor. She had something important to say and she must say it. Laure must hear it . . .

Finally she was able to speak: 'Of course, Laure, I'll help you. I'll help you, Laure dear, I'll help you . . . But how? What can I do?'

'We have to leave. I have to get away from the others. Especially the nutter who closed all the windows. He put fish hooks everywhere. Did you see them? He's paranoid, he's coked up to the gills. He locked me in here, in your room. He gave me dope to keep me quiet.'

'But why did you take it?'

'Because I need it. I'm a user, I told you. I was going to kick the habit, but I was waiting for you to help me. Help me, Elsa. Take me away. I'll tell you everything. I have to get away.'

'That's easy. I haven't even opened my suitcase. The car is in the garage. We'll leave immediately.'

'The car isn't in the garage.'

'Where is it?'

'Orly. I had an accident and I left it there.'

Laure didn't have a driving licence. Elsa didn't ask who had been driving, why they went to Orly, how long she had been taking drugs, who she took them with. She said nothing. She wasn't censoring herself; she said nothing because she had landed in an unknown world where she was an absolute stranger. Even Laure was a stranger to her. She didn't know how one entered this world, how one behaved there, what one said.

Nonetheless she decided. 'Tomorrow morning I'll go and get the car and then we can leave straight away.'

'And I need some Tranxene 50 or I won't be able to stand the withdrawal.'

'That's no problem. I can get some right away.'

'No, tomorrow will be soon enough. I have some codeine I can take in the meantime. I'm going to have a bath and get some sleep. He forced me out of here last night because he knew you were coming back today. But he didn't even realise that the room he locked me into was on the ground floor and gave onto the street. When he left a while ago, he locked the door behind him and I went out the window. He's an idiot.'

'Why did he lock you in?'

'Because of the money. He stole the blank cheques you left for the phone and everything. He didn't want me to go to the bank.'

'I forgot to cross the cheques! Remember, I wrote them at the last minute and I was late. I wanted to call and ask you to cross them, then I decided you'd think of doing it yourself. How many did he take?'

'I don't know.'

Her money! The night classes, the exams . . . a long time

ago, when Laure was still small . . . her first patients . . .
the frantic pace for years to establish herself . . . She earned
a good living now and she was proud of it. She wouldn't
mention it. She knew that it wasn't something she should
bring up now.

'The phone has been cut off.'

'Since when?'

'I don't know. Not too long; I spoke to you the day before
yesterday.'

'It's too bad they didn't disconnect it earlier. That way he
would have had to pay the bill! I told him to pay it . . .
Because he lives on the phone. Before, he was a really minor
dealer, running around all the time. Since he got the cheques,
he's been acting like a big shot. Now he's got people selling
for him. He had his best customers living here . . . that got
on my nerves. That's another reason he locked me in, so I
wouldn't see them. One day I saw one in your office. That
was it – things couldn't go on like that, so I told him . . .'

She talked on and on, telling horror stories without realising it. To her, these were everyday occurrences. Elsa couldn't
understand it. There were also a lot of words she didn't
know. She clung to what she could grasp: that there had
been a lot of people living in the flat, that Laure had been
locked up, that someone she didn't know had his hands on
her bank account. She had to find a way to return to her
own logic, her own vocabulary.

'But why did you let him? It's not like you.'

'He gave me all the stuff I wanted. He was afraid I would
leave, warn you . . . He watched me all the time.'

'Are you afraid of him?'

'No . . . Yes . . . He's mad. He runs on coke, don't you
see? He's crazy. The coke makes him that way. He takes too
much. He's so strung out he doesn't know what he's doing.'

It was as if Elsa's ability to think had begun to atrophy.
Her world was minuscule now. Her existence was reduced
to what Laure was telling her: a story that she found horrifying but that Laure seemed to find commonplace. And yet
Elsa was convinced that there was no other story, that this
horrifying ordinariness was Laure's life, that she must enter
into it. To get closer to her daughter she tried to hold on

to what she knew, what she had seen and guessed, here, throughout the day.

'Were any of them ill?'

'What do you mean, ill?'

'I found vomit everywhere.'

'Some users spew . . . They like it. They say it cleans them out, cleans out their system . . . Heroin screws up your liver . . . But I don't throw up.'

Heroin! She took heroin – the hardest drug of all!

Elsa closed her eyes. Once again she felt she was falling, sliding, that everything was crumbling, that she had no foothold. Perhaps because she hadn't eaten.

'Are you hungry, Laure? I don't think there's anything in the house; I couldn't find anything. But I can go and pick up something to eat from the late-night café. It's open until two or three in the morning.'

'No, thanks. I'm not hungry.'

'You're thin.'

'You think so? No, I'm fine.'

Laure laid her head on the pillow, slipping her arm around her mother's waist. Elsa stared at her: how young she was, how pretty, how little. Laure sighed. 'I could hardly wait for you to come home. What a day it's been!'

Indeed. Laure had no idea what her mother's day had been like, because she had never actually seen the state of the flat. Elsa realised that she had just boarded a moving train, a runaway train. But where was the train coming from? And where was it headed?

If Elsa had known that she was embarking upon a long quest, which, little by little, would eat away not only her understanding but her hopes and goals, would she have refused to help Laure?

That night, the first night, although she didn't know how to deal with the situation, she firmly believed that she would succeed, that she would fix everything, the way she had fixed up the flat.

As a psychologist Elsa had an international reputation. She was passionately interested in other people's bad habits, but she had never had any drug users as patients because she specialised in very young children. She knew from various colleagues that addicts were hard to treat, that in practical terms, the success rate with them was very low, that it was frustrating to work with them – but she would succeed. Laure was right to trust her. She would succeed. It wouldn't be easy, but she would succeed. She would.

Laure ran a bath and locked herself in, though she didn't usually. She knew that Elsa thought that she was beautiful and she was normally quite comfortable parading around in front of her, naked or in skimpy attire that made them both laugh. She often bathed here because the tub was more comfortable than her shower at home. She was usually in a hurry but that didn't stop her having something she had to talk about each time. She would call her mother into the bathroom. Elsa would go and sit in the wicker armchair. Laure would be surrounded by bubbles. They would talk about everything under the sun; they would have serious conversations and burst out laughing every once in a while. They were in it together . . .

But that night Laure locked the door. Everything was different.

Elsa needed some rest. She had to sleep or she wouldn't be able to hold up. She slipped between the sheets and, without even noticing, fell asleep.

The Next Three Days

The Lives of Laure and Elsa over the Second, Third and Fourth Days

The next day withdrawal, or rather the fear of withdrawal, scared Laure off.

The last few days before Elsa's arrival, she had shot up a lot, as if, unconsciously, she had wanted to take full advantage of her mother's absence. That night she slept a long time. She tried to calculate how long it had been since her fix the night before in the bathroom. She didn't know exactly; she didn't know what time it had been then, nor what time it was now. She felt as if it had been a long time. She was cold, and her joints hurt. She told herself she wouldn't wake her mother, she should let her rest, so she decided to go to Chloé's place. The madman – she never wanted to see him again – didn't know Chloé, and she would have codeine, maybe even a Tranxene, or part of a Tranxene, or a Spasmalgine suppository. Anyway, if Chloé did have any smack, she wouldn't take it: that was all over with, she wasn't doing it any more.

Chloé didn't have much, just codeine syrup. Laure emptied the bottle. And then, around four in the afternoon, she went into serious withdrawal. She recognised it although she'd never really experienced it before. It was frightening. She didn't have a penny, and neither did Chloé. Laure took out her address book and started to call the others. Nothing. No one had a thing. Or else they were out, or they were in the same condition as she was. The early afternoon isn't a good time for junkies with no junk. The fear of cold turkey agitates them or paralyses them. The idea of what the torture will be like clutches at their calves, the napes of their necks, their very skins. They become irritable, argumentative, distrustful. No matter how many jumpers they put on, they just cannot get warm.

Laure couldn't go back to her mother's. Something prevented her; she didn't know quite what . . .

She had to find the madman, right away! He was the one with the cheques, the money, everything. But she didn't know the name of the street where he'd taken her the other night. She knew the area, but that was all: near Buttes-Chaumont. She'd never make it. She ran, out of fear.

First she went to a chemist's where an assistant she knew would give her Spasmalgine gratis. He kept the other customers busy while she inserted one immediately, standing up. In exchange she made a date she knew she would never keep. He was pathetic!

Then she took a taxi, stopping at a tobacconist's in the nineteenth *arrondissement*, near the Cameo cinema; that was where she used to score before she had met the madman. 'I'll just be a minute. I have to buy a packet of Marlboros.' The café was smoky, full of people. The driver couldn't see a thing from the outside. She knew; she'd pulled this one before. She opened a door near the toilets; on the other side was a corridor full of dustbins, a grotty glass door, an alley . . . The cab would be waiting a while!

She was in the street, teeth chattering; she ached all over, she was a wreck. The Spasmalgine had stupefied her, the need for heroin exasperated her. People were staring at her. Jerks, the lot of them.

When she finally found the madman it was seven in the evening. Her body, her entire life was torture; she couldn't stand it. She heard him behind the door as it opened.

'You bitch, you little bitch!'

At first she thought he was insulting her because she'd run away. She didn't give a damn. He could say whatever the hell came into his head! She couldn't care less as long as she got a fix.

'I'm sorry. I had to see my mother. It's all over. I've come back. Here I am. But I haven't had a thing all day. I need a fix.'

'I haven't got any smack, so you can't have any, you bitch. It'll do you good to suffer for a while; it'll serve you right!'

'Please . . .'

He ranted, screaming numbers. She figured out that he'd gone to the bank to cash a cheque and hadn't been able to.

'Six thousand francs. That cheque is mine, you made them out to me. There were three cheques for six thousand francs left – eighteen thousand francs! Eighteen thousand francs down the drain! You understand, you stupid cow? What did you tell your mother?'

Laure could see what had happened: Elsa had gone to the bank and stopped the rest of the cheques. So the madman had no money, and no smack!

'I didn't tell her anything! She could easily have found out for herself if she went to the bank. My mother can read; she can count. She doesn't need it all spelt out for her. She figured it out herself.'

'You owe me eighteen thousand francs, get it? Eighteen thousand francs!'

'I don't owe you a thing.'

She backed up into a corner, shaking. She knew she was going to have to fight – and in the shape she was in! For the first time, real withdrawal set in; she could feel it in her bones, in her every cell. What the others had told her about it and what she had imagined were nothing next to what she was feeling. She hated the madman. She could kill him.

'I don't owe you a thing!'

She didn't know why, but it did her good; she began to howl. To howl for the sake of howling. To howl the way a dog howls at death. He grabbed her by the arm and shook her.

'Shut up! We'll have the neighbours breathing down our necks! I've already got the cops on my back. They're out there with their lasers. Christ! I'm surrounded by cops!'

'You're nuts! You've snorted too much coke, that's all. There aren't any cops, there never have been. There weren't any at my mother's and there aren't any here. You're completely strung out, that's all. You're completely paranoid! If you're in that state, you must've found some coke, and you didn't even think of getting any H for me. Who pays for your dope, you bastard?'

'It certainly isn't you. You owe me money.'

She leapt at him. They hit and slapped each other. Laure scratched him, bit him, tried to knee him in the balls. He saw what a rage she was in and tried to protect himself. Finally she ran away.

He couldn't catch her. She was as nimble and quick as an alley cat.

She went back to Chloé's. Chloé had turned two tricks that evening in exchange for smack.

It was pitch-dark out. Paris was calm.

Laure had just shot up. She'd had a rush, and now she was cocooned in a state of total contentment. She was blissful and confident: it would be the last time. Elsa was back; they were going to go away together, and bye-bye dope! She had had it up to here with running around looking for a hit, scrounging for cash, depending on the madman, begging.

And yet in her numbness she knew something, something she couldn't really admit to herself. She knew that she was at the mercy of heroin. She knew it, but she wouldn't admit it. She also had the vague feeling that her mother couldn't do anything for her, because she didn't know enough . . . Would Elsa realise it? Would she learn? And what if she couldn't make it? What if Elsa couldn't help her? It was depressing. Laure knew things her mother didn't. She was tired . . . They would make it, she told herself.

Chloé moved. As usual, she'd nodded off with the spike in her arm. Laure sat up and removed it. She was protective. Chloé was nice: she'd traded half her hit for Laure's mauve sandals. Tomorrow Laure would have to go back to Elsa's barefoot, but that didn't matter; it wasn't far. She pulled the cover up over Chloé and herself. It was warm; it was nice at Chloé's. Chloé sensed her friend's attention, felt for her hand, found it. Chloé's hand was warm in Laure's, like a bird nesting there. Sweet, hand in hand, they drifted deeper into peace.

It was a beautiful day. Yesterday it had seemed as if autumn had arrived, but now it was summer again. It was hot, but a holiday breeze came in through the windows that had been left open all night and blew through the flat.

The bus just went by!

Which bus?

The one that stops outside the flat: the 89!

Paris! Laure! Elsa leapt out of bed. She was still asleep, but already on her feet. The unconscious works a million times faster than the conscious mind. It took scarcely a fraction of a second, just as she awoke, for the events of yesterday to unfold. The whole day in its smallest details, and even memories from before, just before: New York, Kennedy Airport, Roissy . . . She was no longer asleep, she was moving, but she was weighted down with sleep. She was clumsy, she bumped into the bed, she couldn't find her white coat . . . What time was it? She had to unpack; she had to go and get some Tranxene from the chemist's; she had to go to Orly; she had to go to the bank; she had to pay the phone bill. Was Laure still asleep? Elsa shouldn't sleep while Laure was awake. She had to stand watch.

Laure was gone! She had slept in her old room. The bed was unmade. The lamp was on, and underneath it, with the light shining upon it, was a scrap of paper on which she had written 'Back right away' in big letters. Back from where? Where had she gone? Elsa should have woken up earlier; she shouldn't have gone to sleep. And so, on the table in the entrance, she left a note, too: 'Gone for Tranxene and car. Back soon. I love you.'

She dashed around, spoke loudly . . .

At the Orly police station, the officer on duty said, 'Ah, there you are at last! We've been wondering how long we should keep your wreck here.'

Wreck! The car wasn't even six months old! Elsa mustn't let her surprise show. The policeman mustn't guess that she knew nothing of the accident. She must protect Laure at any cost. She began to flutter about like a lady who has done something silly: 'The accident happened just as I was about to take a plane . . . I was late. I was afraid I'd miss my flight. That's why I didn't report it. I was expected in New York . . . I'm still not sure how it could have happened . . . I'm always so careful. I've never even had a ticket.' She stopped and laughed, not knowing where her story was leading, afraid she might have said too much already. She acted scatter-brained, rushed; she couldn't get over how easy it was to lie and put on a show. She wanted the police to think 'Women!' – and that's exactly what they seemed to be thinking, since they soon became protective – and for everything to sort itself out.

'But we sent you a notice.'

'I've only just come back. I didn't have my post forwarded.'

She paid a sum she found astronomical and then saw her beautiful Renault 5 with its metallic grey finish, red seats, radio, and the whole kit and caboodle. Yes, that heap of scrap metal was her car, the most beautiful car she had ever had.

'Be careful on your way back to Paris. I wouldn't be surprised if the steering was out of alignment. Your front wheels . . . You went right smack into the wall, eh?'

'Yes, right smack into it.'

The man shook his head as if to say, 'Women, they're all the same, completely daft.' They both burst out laughing. She was bright and cheerful as could be . . . Fortunately the engine started right away. And off she drove.

The first thing she had seen when she got into the car was a syringe on the floor beside the pedals. She had joked with the police officer and yet had been terrified he would see it, too!

Now she was perspiring so much that her hands slid on the steering wheel. She had trouble turning right; she had to hold on tightly to prevent the car from going left. The steering was definitely out of alignment. She shouldn't be driving the car; it had become a death trap. But she wouldn't leave it in the garage. First she would clean up the mess. The car was like the flat – full of filth and syringes.

It took her two hours to drive home. She rushed up the stairs four at a time, hoping that Laure wasn't growing impatient. Later she'd go and hire a car.

Laure wasn't back!

Elsa didn't feel well. She put it down to running about too much, jet lag, and the fact that she hadn't eaten in a long time – she couldn't remember the last time.

Going to the bank, Orly, hiring a car, eating, having the telephone reconnected . . . Stampeding around in a sweat. A cardboard sandwich scarcely bitten into, thrown away. It was impossible to swallow. She couldn't eat. She was breathing heavily. The nonsense she'd spouted. Everywhere she'd gone, she'd lied: at Orly, the bank, the car hire agency, the post office, the chemist's. And why so effusive? Why such a profusion of fictitious details and invented lives? What made her fabricate such stories? But she had no time to answer such questions, no time to think. She was too busy tearing around, and rushing took the place of thinking. The main thing was to hurry. Between errands she returned home to reassure Laure, but Laure was never there. Each time Elsa left a note on the hall table.

The whole day went by like that. At last the broken-down car was cleaned up and in the hands of a mechanic, a white car was in the parking lot, and in Elsa's handbag, there was Tranxene, a wad of banknotes, even some traveller's cheques. You never could tell . . . A huge amount of money had been spent in six weeks – it was unbelievable! But she mustn't think of that, she mustn't think Laure had spent that much on drugs! What good would it do? Anyway, she didn't know how much drugs cost. What good would it do? She'd promised to help her. She'd manage about the money. She didn't know how, but she'd manage.

The phone rang. How considerate! They had reconnected the line right away.

Elsa had dozed off; she leapt up and ran down the passageway. She hadn't thought to plug in the phone in her bedroom. She hadn't known she would fall asleep; she hadn't thought they would reconnect the line so soon. The telephone company really was very considerate. It was Laure calling, it had to be. She only hoped it hadn't been ringing long. She only hoped Laure didn't hang up.

'Hello.'

'Let me speak to Laure.'

'Laure! She isn't here.'

'Listen, just put Laure on, will you?'

There was such confidence in the voice of the man speaking that Elsa was seized by doubt: maybe she'd been sound asleep without realising it and hadn't heard her daughter come in.

'Just a minute, I'll check.'

The bedroom was empty. Everything was exactly as it had been that morning. The message was still under the lamp: 'Back right away.'

'No, Laure isn't here.'

'Just how stupid do you think I am?'

'I must ask you not to speak to me like that.'

'OK, OK, you're trying to protect your daughter, that's what you're supposed to do. But she won't get away with it, she owes me money, lots of money. She's a real bitch, a little slut . . .'

It was the madman! The one who locked up Laure. He was mad; he talked like a madman. Elsa was trembling. She hung up.

She hung up and then picked the receiver up right away. She was sure the madman would ring again. She had to get a grip on herself. She'd let her emotions get the better of her, but despite his aggressive manner and his insults, she hadn't felt as lost with him as with Laure. He was mentally ill, she could tell just by his voice; she'd heard enough people who were mentally ill. Her daughter was more of a stranger to her than the madman!

Time was different; its rhythm had changed. For two days Elsa had not distinguished between day and night, sleep and wakening. Time no longer seemed to pass as it used to; strangely slow periods alternated with strangely fast periods. All at once she wondered how long she had been standing by the telephone with the receiver off the hook. She was afraid she might put the madman off; she was worried he might decide not to call back, and she quickly replaced the receiver. The line was connected once more.

As she had anticipated, the phone rang again.

'Hello.'

'Look, I'm losing my patience. I knew you'd put the phone back on the hook eventually. I decided to keep ringing until you answered . . . So when are you going to give me my money?'

She took the conciliatory, soothing tone of someone who doesn't want to interrupt but who nonetheless is looking for an opening. She was used to it.

'Excuse me. From what I understand, Laure owes you something, but I don't know what I owe you. Why don't you explain?'

'It's the same. Laure or you, it's the same.'

'In a way, you're right, but it's not exactly the same. You see, I don't know how I come to owe you anything.'

'What's all this rubbish? Listen, it's simple. Your daughter is a junkie and she's greedy, and she's a spoiled brat to boot:

the more you give her, the more she wants . . . Soon she's
going to need a permanent hook-up from the spike to the
spoon . . . Here's the facts: she owes me for her fixes for the
last ten days!'

Never had Elsa listened to a patient the way she was listening to this man. Never had she needed anyone so much. It
hurt to hear him talk about her daughter that way, but it
was also a relief. Now she knew something, at least; she had
some details. She let a certain idea of Laure enter her mind.
And the spoons, she had guessed about the spoons, all those
bent spoons.

'You still there?'

'Yes, I'm listening.'

She acted as if it were all quite natural. In any case she had
just made a decision. 'I'm listening and I think that the best
thing would be if you came round to see me. I'm sure we
can come to some agreement.'

'No, no – I won't go there.'

'Why not?'

'It's full of pigs.'

'What do you mean?'

'Haven't you seen them? They've got the building surrounded! The place is crawling with filth. Whatever you do,
don't touch the fish hooks. Leave everything the way it is!'

He became voluble. He started to rant. He was terrified,
a hunted animal. The pigs were chasing him with lasers; they
had even hit him in the left calf once, and he still had the
mark to prove it.

'And they arrested Sonia downstairs from your flat. She
saw their lasers; she told me. And those three musketeers,
those three creeps, I can't remember their names . . . they
saw the cops the other night in a car parked in Rue de
Vaugirard. I'm not making it up, you know!'

Elsa had fallen back into her listening habits. She got him
to talk. Sentence by sentence she came to understand the
fishing rods, the heaps of furniture in front of the closed
windows. The devastation of the flat was consistent with a
pattern she had never even suspected existed. She learnt as
much as possible: words, addresses, and so on. She knew he
had seen Laure that night. He didn't know where she was

now. He'd looked everywhere for her . . . She got him to tell her that his name was Marcel and that he was twenty-eight. He made a living selling drugs, mainly heroin, but he never touched the stuff himself. He snorted cocaine, but he didn't shoot up.

With the approach of dawn they fell silent. Through the window Elsa could see streaks of ash and lead breaking up the night sky; her strength left her. Marcel became more laconic, wary, as if the new morning alerted him to a new danger. But he no longer knew where the danger lay: with others, himself, or Elsa. He became confused. Again he spoke a little of his mother, who was a concierge in Lyon, a real mother . . .

And then, abruptly, as if the challenge of a new day, of a new beginning, had sprung up before him, threatening him, he had cut off the conversation and there was nothing left but the stubborn signal of the disconnected line. When Elsa hung up, day was about to break. She heard the first bus go by, then the dustmen. Gradually the street came to life. She fell asleep right there on the floor. She didn't even realise that she was falling asleep. Perhaps she thought Marcel would call again.

Beside her was a sheet of paper on which she had written words, drug words. It was a kind of glossary:

spike	fix	dope	heroin
works	hit	drugs	white stuff
shoot up			horse
Harry and Charlie			skag
horse and coke			smack
H and C			gear
rush	fly		brown sugar
	nod off		needle candy
	crash		snow
	down		
speed			hit
			bag
speedy	cool		
clean			
straight			

push

pusher   junkie   gram

deal   junk   quarter

dealer   half

score   high

             stoned   overdose

             zonked   OD

             out of it

cold turkey

WITHDRAWAL

The first thing that went through Laure's mind when she woke up was the Spasmalgine suppositories she had had in her handbag and she reached under the pillow. Phew. They were still there – she'd been afraid for a minute. At Chloé's you had to hide everything, or when you came down you might find someone had stolen the shirt off your back. That's the way things were; you could trade anything for junk. Anything could be worth something, anything could be worth a thousandth of a milligram of junk, of junk dust, you never knew. For example, if you played cards and were winning, you could say to a loser who had a box of Spasmalgine: 'I'll trade you my points for a suppository.' It was a deal like any other, it might work . . . You could always try, you never knew. Four Spasmalgine suppositories were worth something when you had nothing.

Laure realised what a sorry state she was in. She was completely down. She couldn't let Elsa see her like this.

Now that cold turkey was no longer just a scarecrow people shook at her, now that she had actually begun to feel it, she couldn't stop thinking about it, she couldn't stop talking about it. There were a lot of people coming and going at Chloé's. Some came to shoot up; others who had nothing came to try to get somebody to give them something – there were mainly that kind, the poor, shivering ones. Smack was in short supply at Chloé's. They waited. Laure told them about her fight with Marcel, her ordeal. They listened and then told about their experiences. Laure realised she hadn't been through the worst of it yet! She didn't know if she would be able to kick.

There were three or four, maybe five, of them there, waiting in a small corner of the city. A sort of dilapidated nest where Chloé was squatting. A hideaway. A sewer. A haven. A cesspit lined with cushions and ornamental rags. The cracks in the wall held sticks of sandalwood or patchouli, bunches of burnt incense, bristles of yesterday's and the day before yesterday's dreams, witnesses to shimmering highs. Taped to the windows to replace broken panes were pictures of American and English women, men, groups who sang about the people who took refuge here. Glossy images of fabled elders posted to keep out the rest of the world. The pantheon whose legendary withdrawals and overdoses were models for their own humble stories of junkies from the fourteenth *arrondissement*. Wild and wonderful brothers and sisters from California and New York, London and Berlin, with the same veins, the same blood. The words and music of Jimi, Janis, and others played over and over again, day and night, for reassurance, to seal them into the abandoned cell where their lives ticked over. Protective deaths. Veterans released at last from their agony. Tireless night-owls whose round black hearts and long brown veins, spun in endless succession in the hell-hole that the bulldozers had spared, at least for the time being.

Marcel knew nothing of this hideaway; Laure was safe here, where everyone was pure, where there were no madmen hooked on the chimera of cocaine and its bonfires, only pilgrims slowly filing through the snow by candlelight, only the deep and rare sighs of heroin to fan the flames that licked the spoons. At Chloé's, when everyone had a hit and slipped into a private peace, absolute happiness reigned. But that didn't happen often. Here, hash, suppositories, pills and cough syrup were more common than smack. Smack was expensive, very expensive. To get it you had to pull a B & E or turn a trick, and sometimes you just didn't feel like it, you just weren't up to it.

Laure wouldn't admit that she was hooked on heroin; she denied it. Not her, no way. She was a user, not an addict.

The day she decided to quit, she would. But last night she had been facing cold turkey . . .

A little earlier Alex had been by; he had some good stuff, really good. He gave Laure some on credit. He'd known her a long time, since before Marcel. He'd known her back when she'd snorted a little coke, like a rich kid. But Laure wasn't a rich kid, she was a go–getter. Alex liked her; she was stubborn. At one point she was snorting so much that she couldn't sleep. She wanted to do everything at once – film school, sports, music – she spent her nights dancing and singing in clubs, she wanted to start a group, and she wound up being so strung out she couldn't do anything at all. He had been the one to tell her: 'Do a little H, it'll give you balance.' He later heard that she'd followed his advice; she'd moved on to junk and started to shoot up, but he'd lost track of her.

He was pleased to have her as a customer again. He knew that old lady Labbé had money and so he was sure of being repaid. Mothers always paid; fathers were a different story.

'Don't forget to pay me back.'

'Sure thing, Alex. Especially since I'm kicking. This is my last hit, then I'm going back to my mother's. She'll give me the money to pay you, don't worry.'

'Aren't you scared?'

'Yeah, a little bit.'

'Cold turkey throws me into a panic. That's why I can't quit. It scares me shitless.'

'Yeah, I know. The other night I had a rough time. But I can't go on like this.

'I wouldn't be surprised if you did it; you've got guts. It's a good idea . . . The stuff keeps getting more and more expensive . . . and . . . well, anyway, if you change your mind, you know my number.'

'I won't change my mind. I can take it. You'll see. I trained for competition. I was a swimming champ . . .'

'Competition, how bloody stupid! Win, win, win. Win what? What for? First, last, who cares? It's fascist. It's amazing all the rubbish they put in our heads . . .'

'It's nuts! Hours and hours doing lengths. The chlorine

burns your eyes and dries out your hair. And the coach – what an idiot! All that for a medal, and it's not even gold!'

'All that to teach you to obey, you mean. To send you into the army, to war, "one–two, one–two, about face, right, left!" as if they were sending you to buy a sack of potatoes . . . What I want is a great big bike, you know, the latest Yamaha . . .'

'Like the ones we saw at the Bastille last year? Remember?'

'Yeah, like that, but the latest model.'

'Come off it! Don't make me laugh!'

'Well I'm telling you, Laure, if I had one, I'd get the hell out of here. I'll take you if you want. We could go to a beautiful sunny beach.'

'Yeah. In the Bahamas.'

'Where's that?'

'I don't know. It's great, though. I've seen pictures.'

'Right, well, that's where I'd go. I'd lay me down under a coconut palm, and in Paris you wouldn't hear another word about little old Alex, let me tell you. If I could just get the hell out of here . . . *Ciao, au revoir*, and goodbye France!'

'Wait, wait! I hear Chloé coming in. Hand over the junk, I don't want to give her any. She exploits me, she takes advantage of everything. She nicked my mauve sandals last night. That bitch would rip off her own grandmother.'

'She's nice enough, though.'

'She bugs me. I don't want to give her any.'

'Here, then. Well, I've got to be off.'

'Where to?'

'Around. I dunno.'

Alex hustled at the Drugstore Saint Germain, Laure knew. He made no secret of it; everyone knew. She had Elsa, and he had a bunch of sugar daddies, or snowmen, as he jokingly called them.

Fatigue and anxiety had sapped Elsa's resistance. She had eaten nothing, or next to nothing, since she'd been back. Perhaps it was the lack of food that made her cry continuously; she was a hunted animal, and now she was being devoured by the very thing she was fleeing. She needed help, she needed to talk to someone – it was all too much for her. But what was happening to her was too private, too deep. Who could she share it with? She wasn't tempted to call her parents. It would hurt them; their disappointment would be unbearable. They had such confidence in her; they were so proud of her, so proud of Laure.

She thought of Jacques all the time. It was as if he were there . . . He had been twenty-two when he died, the same age as she had been, the same age as Laure was now. But what was the use? He was dead and she couldn't bring him back to life.

Often she curled up on the bed. The ordeal had purged her, swept away her underpinnings. She was fragile, docile, easy to take, as she had been in the beginning . . . Jacques had been very tall, blond and slim. He moved and spoke as a free man. He smelled of freedom; it was his scent. Some days, when he seemed to be getting away from her, she had the impression that he reeked of freedom: the smell of the night streets that he walked with long strides because it was cold out and he never had enough to pay for the Métro. He was a dangerous alley cat, but sweet. They loved each other.

And then right away, too soon, came a child and the war. The war and letters. What a war! What letters!

He wrote non-stop from wherever he was, from the rocky slopes of Kabylia, from rest camp, in the midst of the lads boozing or snoring . . . He wrote on whatever paper he could find, sometimes even across Elsa's letters; it was hard to read. At first he wrote that he was going to run away to South America and would send for them: 'If not for you, I'd clear out today.' Later, as time went by, less and less of what he wrote concerned her. All he wrote about was military idiocy, colonial concupiscence, cretinous power, bestial power, imbecilic power. There was no longer anything, or hardly anything, about her or their child, only an affectionate closing just above the signature, *Jacques* all by itself, with not even an underscore or a flourish.

One day they told her he was dead. She didn't ask how it had happened. Killed, that was all.

Jacques's death. She had prowled around it for a few weeks . . . not even that, a few days, a fortnight . . . and then she had escaped. Once her mother-in-law had said to her: 'You don't seem to have mourned my son very long.'

She had looked for work. There was no question of being taken care of by her family, of playing the widow in Aix with her baby . . . Jacques had never liked anyone to help him; he had been independent. She would raise her daughter independently. That was the reason she had given for going back to Paris: she would raise Jacques's daughter independently. She had found a job as a secretary and started to take courses again, at night, by correspondence. It had taken her a while but she had earned her degrees. First she had practised in a welfare clinic, then with a colleague. Subsequently she had opened her own office. Patients began to come. She developed her method, the 'Labbé method' – what François respectfully called 'your scribbling method'. Every day she had found her work more interesting. Laure was an easy child. She was no trouble at all.

She hadn't thought enough about Laure, she had thought too much about herself. And she had not gone into mourning for Jacques.

It was bound to happen; it had to explode. Other people made such an effort to build a life for themselves! But she hadn't made much of an effort; at least, she wouldn't have said so. She would rather have said that she had managed the best she could and everything had worked out . . . Yet she had to be punished one day; someday something had to happen, something awful.

Elsa closed her eyes. Her tears formed a fine shiny film as they dried, irritating her cheeks and the corners of her mouth.

She rubbed her face. Despite her fatigue, she knew she wouldn't sleep. She would curl up with her sorrow and her mistakes, exhausted, beaten, waiting for Laure. There was nothing else for her to do.

She was floating. She wasn't really there. She was just lying there.

A little girl of eight was going to confession, all alone, in the cathedral next door to her house in Aix. The side aisle, paved with large stones, was a covered street where her slightest movement made an echo. She was so young, so small, how could she make so much noise, be so important? A chill fell on her shoulders and she felt as if it were pushing her into the granite. She felt fragile, insignificant, compared with the columns she was passing that held high their weighty capitals. The confessional was far off at the other end of the nave, behind the chancel. She advanced in the empty darkness with its heavy smell of incense and stagnant water. In the solitude, a chair squeaked, a throat was cleared, a sigh escaped. Were there people there? She couldn't see them. Were the stones alive? Why did she have to go to confession when it was such a nice day? At the end of her dreadful journey would be the litany of her sins. She would confess; she would tell how she was capable of filching fried doughnut batter, how she willingly went along with the little boy from downstairs who took her by the hand in the stairwell, how she would rather look at the tree in the garden than tidy her room, how she would yawn on purpose while her grandfather was speaking at table, because he annoyed her, how she would act innocent when her mother then gave her a severe look. She was a wicked, greedy, disrespectful liar and a hypocrite!

She knew that Laure wasn't coming home, that she was somewhere in the city, somewhere else, somewhere where she was both lover and prey.

Where was Laure? What could she be doing all this time? Elsa's mind was racing at a thousand words a second, her thoughts a whirlwind behind her closed eyelids and lips.

She glanced at the alarm clock often to make sure that time was passing. If not for the hands that moved a little, she would never have known it. To her, time had stopped. Laure had been gone a long while now. It was night. Fortunately it was night. There was no need to lie. Offices were closed. The streets were empty.

Laure was caught up in heroin; she was under its spell, bewitched by it. She was reasonable, though; she wanted to stop shooting up, and she would stop – each new hit was the last.

One more and that's it; I haven't got any more money. One more and that's it; I won't be afraid of cold turkey. Just this one, and that's it; I'll be in good enough shape to go back to my mother's.

After that last one she would go back to Elsa's and she would be rid of it all. She'd have no problem with kicking, no problem with money. She trusted her mother; Elsa would fix everything, just like she used to.

Ever since Laure had become hooked, she no longer measured time in days or hours; she measured it in hits. Time consisted of one hit after another, and between one hit and another there was virtually no time, just a rush, a few moments. The rest of her existence was not time, it was a slow descent, it was starting to think about the next hit, it was running around after some smack with withdrawal on her heels. A hit, listlessness, anxiety, distress, another hit . . . It passed quickly.

Laure did not realise quite how quickly. She hadn't been an addict long, just since the summer. Before she met Marcel, she used to shoot up once in a while, out of bravado, for fun, never out of need. She had never been aware of how voracious, how demanding heroin was.

Now heroin was in her blood; she was hooked. She was trapped in a separate world, one with its own internal logic and constraints so powerful that she had forgotten what it was like outside. She had no idea what Elsa was going through; she simply could not imagine it. She didn't know that three days had gone by.

During those three days Elsa didn't know how to deal with time. She was dependent on her daughter, who was not there, who was lost, who was perhaps dead. How could she endure the stagnation, the powerlessness?

Her ignorance and impotence in the face of this emptiness were so great that sometimes she even considered turning to the police, reporting Laure missing so they would look for her, help find her. But she didn't do it. Her long conversation with Marcel had taught her about a parallel world ruled by other laws. The police were exactly like her and could do nothing more than she could. Neither she nor the police was in Laure's world; both were outside the laws Laure lived by. That was the only thing Elsa knew now; she knew there was another world in Paris, but she didn't know where it was or how to get there.

So she continued to organise, put things away, clean up. This time she went at the flat calmly, obstinately, as she had gone at her research and everything else in her life. In this meticulous, systematic, almost academic, industrious, yet curious way of hers, she tried to discover how the drug addicts who had lived in her flat had been organised, and attempted to guess at their rhythms, their needs. She grew accustomed to the idea that she would be living in a world with this logic and this will. But what logic? What will? She was going to have to learn and understand, if she wanted to be able to help Laure.

Elsa had helped a great many children that way, by entering into their disorder. But she entered into it only for the duration of the sessions at her office or the clinic, and then in the calm of her office while she examined the information provided by each patient. Now, however, to help her daughter, she would have to enter into Laure's disorder twenty-four hours a day. The disorder would become her order. It would be her full-time job. That was her plan. If she went about it any other way, if she tried to continue her work and save her daughter at the same time, she wouldn't do a good job of either. She knew herself. She had to choose between her work and her daughter, between herself and Laure. She chose Laure.

During the three days, as she was making preparations for her absence, she let her life go; and left to itself, it came to a sudden halt. She acted instinctively. Sometimes she thought she was going mad, but that didn't change her determination. The existence that she had created for herself stopped there, because she couldn't go on with it.

She called Professor Greffier to tell him she was temporarily interrupting her work with him. She gave no explanation. He insisted on having one. She was curt, saying that she would drop by to see him as soon as she could, but she didn't know when that would be.

She referred her patients to a colleague, a woman who followed her research step by step, a sort of disciple. She told her she was taking a sabbatical: 'I need to study further before going back to my patients. I don't know if I'll be staying in Paris or if I'll go somewhere else. I don't want to be tied to a schedule.'

She called in Jacqueline, her secretary, and told her the same story. She said that in three months, according to the work plan she was going to draw up, she would either begin seeing her patients again or Jacqueline would be free to look for another job. Together they set up a system of telephone answering machines: one at Elsa's to forward calls to Jacqueline's, and another at Jacqueline's. There would be papers to sign. She would ring and leave messages; she didn't know where she would be.

Jacqueline knew Elsa well and didn't believe a word of what she was saying, but she asked no questions. She was upset. They had been so close, understood each other so well, worked so well together. She took away the appointment book and what was left of the files. She wondered what had happened over the holidays to cause such disruption. But she asked no questions about that, either. She took everything, moved the whole office; it took three trips. Elsa was heartbroken. She drove nervously, without speaking. It was as if she wanted to show Jacqueline the door, get rid of her as quickly as possible. At the last moment Jacqueline asked, 'Is there anything I can do for you?' Elsa shook her head and drove off right away. She was afraid she would burst into tears and when it was all over she was relieved: she was free.

She read everything possible and imaginable about drugs and drug addicts. Under the pretext that she had a case, she called colleagues and learnt that only a tiny percentage of heroin addicts ever manage to quit. Tiny: two per cent, said one; five per cent, said another. Only one said twenty per cent. She would do it. She clung to her conviction.

She still had many things to think about – money, especially. How long would she be away? She had no idea. How long could she manage without working? Two years, if she were careful. Maybe four years, if she sold Laure's flat. Thank goodness for the bequest from her old aunt in Marseilles!

At first the telephone rang often. On the other end of the line were hesitant voices, speaking too slowly, making an effort to be articulate, polite.

'I'd like to speak to Laure, please.'
'Laure isn't here.'
'Is Marcel there, then?'
'Marcel isn't here, either.'
'Is Sonia there?'
'I don't know a Sonia.'
And after a pause, 'Who're you?'
'Laure's mother.'
'Sorry to bother you.'

After two days the phone stopped ringing, or almost. Elsa realised that Laure's world had closed up. She was sorry. She blamed herself for being brusque at first; she should have got them to talk. Now, whenever anyone rang, she tried to sound receptive, but it didn't work. She began to feel a certain sympathy for Marcel, at least . . . But he didn't call. Had he found Laure?

She thought of nothing but that, of things like that; her own life was no longer of any interest to her. She had settled her affairs, that was all over with, that was before. She wanted to save her daughter, that was what she kept telling herself. She didn't analyse the situation beyond that point. Why else would she be acting as she was? For whom? Not for herself, in any case. She was in great shape, well balanced . . .

She no longer went out, no longer phoned anyone.

Never in her whole life had Elsa really waited. She had expected a child, waited for examination results, queued at the butcher's and baker's, waited for a bus or train, but the duration of those waits had always been predictable. She had only had to wait, and it was all over in six months, two weeks, five minutes – it just took a little patience. Now she was waiting as she had never waited before. She awaited everything.

The apartment was in order. There wasn't a speck of dust left anywhere. There was nothing more to do. They would leave as soon as Laure got back. This time she wouldn't go to sleep.

She was in a no-man's-land, an intermediate zone between two lives. She couldn't stay there long.

She had no grip on the future because she didn't know what she was waiting for. She was struggling in a void, fighting against nothing. And when she realised that becoming agitated wouldn't do any good, Laure's absence loomed even larger and her death seemed a real possibility. She knew that all it took was one shot too many.

During the fourth night, because the silence and inactivity were destroying her and she couldn't stand it any longer, she suddenly thought of François. She hadn't thought of him since she'd been home. They hadn't known each other long, and didn't see each other often, but it seemed as if they had always known each other. There was a certain complicity and tenderness between them. They were both loners, and being together was like playing a trick on their habits; they pretended to be a couple, to live as a couple, and it made them laugh. She must have been quite overwhelmed to have forgotten François like that. It was evening in New York, so he might be home; the timing was good. The idea of ringing him filled the void.

She settled in with her packet of cigarettes and an ashtray, placing the telephone beside her on the bed. She knew the number by heart. To hell with the expense! Anyway there was a reduced rate for night calls. She dialled; the line was engaged. A good sign; it meant he was home. Americans and their phones! What would they do without them?

She remembered a huge poster in the arrival area of the

Dallas airport: a photograph of a cowboy in a telephone box, standing in a very nonchalant, sexy way. He was absorbed in conversation, and you could tell he was in the midst of seducing a woman or closing a good business deal. At the bottom of the poster it said in big red letters: 'When I'm not on a horse, I'm on the phone.' It was an ad for telephones . . .

Elsa shrugged. She wondered if it was a good idea to call François. She dialled again; it rang in New York, and immediately she heard the voice of François, close.

'Yeah.'

'Hello, François.'

'Oh, hi, Elsa! How are you? What time is it there?'

'Two in the morning.'

'Jet lag is keeping you up and you thought of good old François, right? Did you have a good trip back?'

'Fine, as usual. Nothing special.'

'How's Paris? Is the weather good?'

'Yes, I think so. I think it's fine.'

'You're not sure?'

'Not really. And it's dark out right now.'

'I'll bet they were happy to see you at the lab. Old Professor What's-his-name has a real soft spot for you.'

'Professor Greffier. I haven't been to the lab.'

'What? But that's the first thing you wanted to do!'

'I'm having a few problems.'

'What's the matter?'

'It's my daughter.'

'Laure?'

'That's right, Laure. I've only got one daughter!'

'OK. You're upset.'

'No, I'm not upset, I'm . . .'

She began to cry. She didn't want to, but she cried and couldn't stop.

'Come on, Elsa, baby. You know children are nothing but a pain in the ass.'

Since he'd been living in the States, he'd adopted an accent and way of speaking that Elsa normally liked a lot, but that night it irritated her. She didn't feel like being called baby.

'You haven't got any children; you've no idea what it's like.'

'OK, but I'm a psychiatrist. You've forgotten I'm a shrink, and we shrinks know everything, or guess everything.'

He was joking, but his attempt at cheerfulness was painful to her, because it was so far from what she was feeling. She was annoyed with him for his jokes and with herself for being unable to laugh. She shouldn't have called.

'François, don't make fun. I'm very unhappy.'

'Elsa, baby, what's going on?'

'Don't call me baby. She takes drugs, François, she takes heroin.'

'Does she inject it?'

'Yes.'

'That's serious, Elsa, really serious. You want some advice?'

'Yes, I don't know what to do any more.'

'Forget it.'

'What do you mean?'

'Protect yourself. We have no solutions for drug addicts. Just forget about the whole thing. If you don't, you'll wind up getting hurt.'

'But she's my daughter, I can't just forget about her. I can't do that.'

'How old is she?'

'Twenty-two.'

'She's not a kid any more. It's her life. Don't get mixed up in it.'

'She could die!'

'Yeah, it's too bad, but think about yourself. You have to be callous or you'll die, too. I'm sorry to be talking to you this way, but you're not a little girl, either. You're a capable woman, Elsa. A very capable woman. Many people need you, that's what counts. That's all that counts. At the conference everyone said that your paper was the most important of the whole bunch. Your research on entropy is first-rate stuff! Entropy, increasing disorder – we're all obsessed with it. We're all trying to reduce or control disorder. Now we're waiting for you to publish something and you're going to do it. That's the one thing you have to do.'

The last conference had been in Sydney, just before the holidays. And what a trip it had been! Straight there and back. Australia, the conference, her observations, her findings – it all seemed so remote now. It was all so remote. Remote was not the term; lost, rather, astray, diverted, in inconceivable disarray.

'My paper was academic, boring and pretentious. I wanted to appeal to that lot of cretins; I wanted to show them . . . I don't even know what I wanted to show them. In Sydney I tossed a bottle into the ocean but the bottle was empty.'

'Cut it out, Elsa! I'm telling you your entropy theory is great!'

'It is not. Thermodynamics is thermodynamics and the psyche is the psyche. My work is nothing but scientism, plain and simple. I'm a century out of date!'

'Elsa, don't start that again. We discussed it all summer. The fascinating thing is linking entropy, or psychological disorder, whatever you want to call it, with local hormonal secretions. You know very well what the discovery of endorphins has meant – you talked about it yourself.'

'Every day someone discovers a new natural substance that may change the way the body works, every day! What am I getting mixed up in? Tell me! Entropy will never be controllable. Neither its quantity nor quality will ever be predictable. I don't know anything! I'm nothing but a fraud!'

'You're not being honest with yourself. Snap out of it. Keep on with your research. You can't quit now. I'm waiting for you to publish and you're going to do it. It's the one thing you have to do.'

She let him talk, not listening. If he only knew how far gone she was already. If he only knew about the scattered, dirty files she had thrown away. If he had only seen Jacqueline leave with the card file. She hung up after promising to get some rest.

'Yes, I'm going to get some sleep, François. Yes, I feel better now. I'm going to bed. You go to bed, too. Sleep well. I'll call you again soon.'

She was sure she wouldn't call him again. She had severed all her ties with him. She didn't know why, she just knew it was necessary.

She stretched out on the bed. She thought of the cottages you rent in the summer. You spend the last day putting things away, putting everything back the way it was, erasing all traces of yourself, your habits, your accidents, so the place is the way it was before, anonymous, vacant. It was as if you were cleaning up your very life, packing it into suitcases and bags to make off with it like a thief. You acted like an intruder; the place became progressively more foreign to you. And then came the moment when the blinds and then the door had to be shut, and you had to leave. The house stayed behind. You had lived in it, given it a bit of memory, had a relationship with it, but it was over. The need to leave was greater. It was over.

Elsa was on her bed; at least, it looked as if she were there. She had put on a travelling outfit: grey trousers, white blouse, red pullover and socks. But that was only the way it looked. She herself was like a polluted haze clinging to a city.

Later, much later, when it was all over, Elsa would remember the three days that she had waited for Laure as a necessary time, an opportunity. She was fortunate to have had those three days. And she would tangle up the passage of those days with an old, happy memory of ice wagons.

When she had been a child in Provence, people had said that it took the soul three days to leave the body after death.

It was during the war, in the midst of an August heat wave, and a woman in the house across the street had died. Through the front window Elsa had watched men with hooks unloading beautiful steaming blocks, long bars of clear ice with an opaque centre, from a pile on the back of a horse-drawn cart. They slid them along, then deftly balanced them on their shoulders, which were covered with a jute sack folded in four, and off they went. It was so hot that the ice began to melt right away, dripping onto the cobble-stones and pavement, making it look as if it had rained. They needed a lot. 'In this heat, a body decomposes in a few hours,' her mother had said. They brought it steadily, morning and evening.

The little girl in the freshly polished room that smelt of violets was reminded regularly by the bell in the shop that her parents were in good health and that business was brisk. Settled into her observatory, sheltered in provincial comfort, she watched the men working and imagined that the frozen soul of Madame Bouleng was leaving her body through all its orifices. The soul had to rise bit by bit, iridescent, an icy ghost. At the right moment, when the coffin was being taken to the cemetery three days later, the soul would leave its owner's thick lips, long ears and hooked nose forever, to fly off into a blue paradise, a ravishing creature escorted by angels with crystal voices. For all that time, those three days, the little girl, enchanted by the radiant metamorphosis that was taking place before her, had not left the window . . .

But while she was waiting for Laure, Elsa didn't remember that. She didn't know there would be three days. She knew nothing. She had no idea where Laure was.

The Fifth Day

On the morning of the fifth day, Laure was back!

Elsa woke up and heard her in the kitchen, making breakfast as she had done thousands of times before.

In the morning, in the kitchen making breakfast – it was Laure!

Elsa ran down the passageway and stood by the table. Laure was sitting; she had taken out Melba toast, butter, and jam, and warmed up yesterday's coffee. She knew that her mother was there but didn't look at her.

'Isn't there any bread?'

'No, I didn't buy any . . . You were gone a long time.'

' "A long time." You're always exaggerating. I went to see a girlfriend, that's all.'

'But three days . . .'

'Three days! Come on, jet lag has thrown you all off.

Three days! And anyway, don't start keeping track of how long I'm out like you did when I was a teenager . . . Are we leaving, then?'

'Whenever you want. Everything's ready. I've hired a nice new white car. I've got your Tranxene. I've got some money. We're all set.'

'Where are we going?'

'I thought we could drive down to the Midi, towards the sun.'

'To Aix!'

'No, not Aix. A hotel. But we can go somewhere else if you'd rather.'

'No, no, that's fine. Sunshine, a hotel . . . I'll eat up, change and then we can leave. Great!'

Listening to Laure, Else realised that she wasn't talking the way she used to. It wasn't so much her words as her sentence structure and her tone. There was something cocky in her voice when she spoke, something coarse and crude, but there was a weariness about it, too. Marcel had sounded the same the other night.

Learning words. Elsa remembered learning the jargon of her profession, quite late in life.

She had met Jacques shortly after finishing *lycée*. She had started studying psychology to be with him at university, but she had abandoned it when Laure had been born soon afterwards. Back then, she'd used the language that young women, young mothers, use. And then Jacques had died. She'd taken up her studies again. Suddenly other words, the words of her future profession, had become part of her life. At first she didn't even dare say them; she felt they didn't really suit her. Sometimes she heard herself speaking and it sounded ridiculous, farcical. But the words gave her power, they showed she had degrees; they made her different, they made her superior. So she used them – until she realised that they were masks to hide ignorance, that they could also frighten, that using them all the time wasn't the sign of a good psychologist. Now that she was accustomed to them she used them only when absolutely necessary. The terms were valuable tools; she didn't overuse them. She often said, 'It bothers me to think I might be a latter-day Diafoirus.'*

Elsa was wary of how people used words. That was partly why she had chosen to specialise in young children. What they had to express was just as complex as adults, but they didn't yet know how to hide behind the words they knew. Their babblings were often clearer than their parents' speeches.

Elsa was very adaptable, able to blot herself out in order to understand another person. She had believed that this ability gave her a special aptitude for psychology and a special aptitude for love. She had believed that she loved each child she helped because she let herself be guided by what the child expressed, because she let herself absorb it. She began by saying little so as not to frighten the patient with her own words, and paid attention only to the child's linguistic quirks, preferences for certain phrases, certain pictures, or, on the contrary, the complicated roundabout ways of speaking that the child used to avoid certain words or images. She was especially interested in scribbles, in what was not clearly expressed, not articulated. She didn't begin to intervene until she felt she could discern where the child was losing its energy, where disorder was entering its mind. Only then would she introduce different words, or the usual words with another meaning, which would make their way in the child's brain and perhaps help it to progress. She used to believe that she did it out of love, love for her work and love for the child. Until she found herself confronted with Laure's case, Laure's disorder.

This morning in the kitchen, Laure's words and verbal tics hinted at a world that Elsa found unbearable. She wasn't sure she had enough love to enter into it, enough love for her daughter. She was no longer sure of anything. She no longer had any confidence in herself. She no longer knew why she had been so enthusiastic about her work. While her mind told her to flee, her instincts told her to stay.

* The name of a father and son who were both ignorant, pretentious physicians in *Le Malade Imaginaire* by Molière.

Her instincts made her stay, her instincts and a memory: her father, on Sundays, near Carpentras, hiding with her in thickets of broom or bramble close to a linden tree whose leaves made an almost perfect green sphere against the sky. Her father was superb at imitating bird sounds: their trills, coos, cheeps. He had learnt how to do it as a child, and through diligent practice and determination, he had perfected his technique so that now he could sing as if he were a bird himself.

He strung up some grey netting from the store between two dead branches under the tree. To prop up the net, he used a third forked branch with a long cord leading back from it to their hiding place. Beforehand, he had made a nest of twigs and placed a decoy in it under the netting. He whistled and whistled, and the birds came: titmice, gold-finches, sparrows, drawn by the cheery calls of their false friend. It was thrilling. They hopped, beat their wings, kicked up dust. Her father went on whistling. You had to wait until there were lots of them, until the net was teeming with them, before pulling the cord. But you couldn't wait too long, or they would all take flight at once for no discernible reason, and wouldn't return. Her father knew exactly when to pull. He would tug the cord sharply and skilfully, and the net would fall. Then the two of them would run and throw the squawking, struggling birds into a sack.

Elsa genuinely loved these hunting parties, and thought there was nothing better than the little birds they roasted on a spit over an open fire in the evening.

She sat down opposite her daughter. She looked at Laure, who had stopped talking and was absently chewing mouthfuls of toast and butter.

'You aren't hungry.'

'No, but I have to eat. Elsa, please don't watch me like that!'

Laure felt hunted, and she wanted to run away. She no longer understood why she was there. She couldn't bear her mother's worried attention. That wasn't what she had come for. It was Elsa's strength and competence she was looking for, but what she saw this morning was a woman at bay, kept at bay by her. Under those conditions, it wouldn't work. She might as well leave again straight away.

She imagined that Elsa would be unable to catch up with her, that they would never find each other, that she'd made a big mistake. She blamed herself; she never should have asked Elsa for help.

'Don't act like such a narc!'

Narc? What did that mean? Had it anything to do with narcotics? Elsa wasn't sure; she'd never heard the word before. She had only a second or two, three at most, to pick up on it. How could she choose so quickly between an angry retort, an intelligent reply, a clever comeback, attentive silence . . . Her mind was blank; she improvised. She shut her eyes – at least she could hide her gaze so that doubt, anger, and disgust in her wouldn't show. She put her foot on the chair rung, leant an elbow on the table, and let it slide, resting her chin on it. She sprawled on the sand, in other words. She sprawled on a meadow, a carpet of pine needles. Yes, that was it, she was stretched out on thyme-scented scrubland She didn't rush; she was nonchalant.

'Narc, narc – that's easy to say, isn't it? Very funny.'

Well, that was it, she had somehow managed to get the ball back into Laure's court. Her answer had been completely meaningless, but at least she had answered. She hadn't cut the lines of communication.

Laure saw her mother stretched out at the table, her arms tanned, her hands covered in freckles. She loved the woman she saw. She loved her weathered skin, her autumn colours. Her mother was like a blazing fire after a long walk through dead leaves, in the October light, after school had started again.

'How were your holidays?'

'Fine, but at the end I wanted to come home.'

Elsa opened her eyes and looked at Laure. And kept on looking at her. Love flowed back into her of its own accord; she could feel it spreading through her body and mind.

'I wanted to see you. I missed you.'

But she had never imagined that her daughter's homecoming would be like this: she, Elsa, asleep, and Laure so touchy.

And to think that occasionally during the three days she had even dreamt of what a happy reunion it would be.

Feeling the warmth and tenderness in her mother's gaze, Laure began to relax; maybe they would make it, after all. She stared at her thin fingers fiddling with the toast and butter and saw a needle puncture on the back of her hand. She remembered her first fix. She hadn't been able to give herself the injection. The syringe had been an insurmountable obstacle: it had disgusted and frightened her. She had been annoyed with herself for being so scared, for not hazarding the step that would set her apart from the junk groupies who cloaked themselves in its mysteries, charms and dangers but never dared explore them . . . In the end, a girl she didn't even know had tied her off. She had seen the needle nuzzle up against the swollen blue vein in the crook of her arm, then slowly slide in, like the tip of a hot knife into butter. The girl had drawn out a little blood with the plunger. Laure had watched as tendrils of red swirled slowly through the liquid, darkening it, and panic had gripped her; perhaps she made an attempt to escape, a feeble attempt, but the girl had pushed all the way . . . It hadn't taken long, virtually no time at all, for ecstasy to burst into bloom like those Japanese flowers in a shell that open up when dropped into water, freeing tissue-paper treasures. Corollas dilated, spreading their spectacular multi-coloured petals. Immediately – instantaneously – Laure became a tree, and a warm breeze caressed her, down to her tiniest branches, her tiniest leaves. Contentment flowed to the tips of her deepest, most hidden roots. She was bliss itself. Everything was so warm, so soft. The first rush.

It was never that good again.

Today, it wasn't even the remembrance of that rush that made her yearn for the next hit. It was . . . She didn't know what . . . She wouldn't admit what.

'I'm not hooked, you know. I just have to quit because junkies are dogs and I never want to get like that.'

'Why do you call them dogs?'

'Because they beg, they're sly. They're double-crossers.'

Laure had been afraid of dogs ever since she'd been bitten

one summer in Aix when she was small. At the time she hadn't kicked up a fuss, and no one would have thought she had been frightened. And yet, ever since, she had had an unreasonable fear of dogs.

'Do you have the Tranxene?'

'Yes, do you want some?'

'No, not yet. I have to try to hold out. The worst is over.'

'What do you mean?'

'The first twenty-four hours are the worst. Then it's hard for another three days. Well, the first week is hard. Don't worry, I'll be all right.'

Say nothing, say nothing. And above all, don't ask questions. Don't be indiscreet. Don't stare. Act as if nothing is happening. We're going on holiday. We're going to enjoy ourselves!

It was late September, almost October, when they left for the Midi. They were going away. There was nothing more to it than that. They were going away at a time when most people were coming back, that's all. Factories were running at full force again, playgrounds were bustling with children again, the Métro was packed again. They were going away: they were leading a life of ease, *la dolce vita*. They were exceptional.

From birth Elsa's life had been set to the rhythm of bells, calendars, chimes, dates, buzzers, birthdays, tick-tocks, noises and silences – cadenced time that controlled her freedom. She had never tried to escape. Quietly, obstinately, she had developed her own tempo based on those rhythms.

Elsa didn't like open conflict but she was subversive. That was why wandering minds attracted her, because wandering minds disturb the order within, knock over signposts, ignore them, can force them to change without attacking them directly. There was something contradictory about Elsa: she didn't like order, but she didn't like to be noticed, either. Leaving at a time when most people were returning home therefore made her feel exposed, and she didn't like it. The idea of heading south in a white car in the middle of the day in late September was shocking.

Unlike her mother, Laure liked to provoke, to confront

people. She liked to stand out, be excessive, beat records, be first or last. Demonstrations counted for a lot with her: she needed to cross swords, to test and be tested. To her, the idea of heading south in a white car in the middle of the day in late September, her body full of drugs, was fun.

'I can't find my nice frock.'

'Which one?'

'The pink one . . . with the grey-blue pattern . . . you don't know the one I mean.'

'I haven't seen anything that looks like that. I washed and ironed everything wearable and put it in your chest of drawers.'

'Yeah, I saw. That's all ugly stuff, it's not mine.'

'Your things must be at your place.'

'No, there's nothing left there.'

'I put heaps of rags and things in bags I was going to take down to the rubbish bins when we left.'

'Where are they?'

'In the cupboard by the front door.'

'I'm going to look for it.'

There was a flurry of activity in the flat. The two women moved about impatiently, preparing for the trip.

Elsa with the suitcases: one for Laure, one for herself.

Laure with the dark green plastic bags, knotted twice, firmly.

Elsa was methodically packing shoes and stacks of folded clothes.

Laure was losing her patience with the tight knots.

Elsa was in her room, Laure in the hall.

'I can't get these things undone!'

'Then tear them, there are plenty more . . . Don't toss stuff everywhere. I don't feel like cleaning the house again before we leave.'

Elsa and her need for order!

Laure began to rummage through the ripped bags. She pulled out a jumper tangled up with stockings . . . pulled out something else . . . Her movements were agitated, interrupted before they were finished; unfinished gestures that strewed clothing about her. And when anything resisted she

57

tugged at it until it tore. She wanted that frock, she wanted it above all else. She yelled, 'Have you thrown anything out?'

'No clothes.'

Laure whined but kept hard at it. An unpleasant smell emanated from the pile of rags and reached Elsa. It was the stink of that first day: vomit, something burnt, mustiness, filth, something sour, mixed with incense, sandalwood, patchouli, Chanel No. 5 . . . Laure had been living in it for weeks; it didn't bother her; to her it was normal. At least it didn't smell like Ajax.

Elsa had finished packing. In the hall, she looked at her daughter, who hadn't heard her coming. She didn't recognise her. Those were Laure's limbs, her face; she recognised the smallest details of her features, her movements, the way her shoes had shaped to her feet. She recognised all that, and yet she didn't recognise her daughter. A substitution had been made; that wasn't Laure there, but someone who looked like her.

Five days earlier, standing in the half-light gazing at her ransacked apartment, Elsa had known that she could not avoid entering it. Today she knew that she could not avoid leaving on a trip with this stranger.

She looked closely at Laure, seeing in her body and expressions many signs that she had never seen before. Irrationally, she felt that Laure was possessed, that the devil was in her, that the devil existed. She couldn't stand the thought. She couldn't stand herself thinking that. It was an unacceptable regression; it nullified all that she had done to become responsible and active and competent. And yet the conviction that the devil existed remained; only absolute evil could have changed her daughter to this point. Elsa could break free of this absurdity only by saying to herself with all her heart: 'I hate heroin!' The reality of her hate was so strong she clung to it as to a lifebuoy. Never had she experienced so intense and wicked a feeling. 'I hate heroin.'

For five days Elsa's life had been in upheaval, and she was exhausted. She was overwhelmed by what was happening, and yet inside it was as though she had been expecting it all, as though there were a place in her set aside for it, and also a place in Laure, and a place at home. As if everything had been prepared all along for this departure, this hell!

The only thing that kept her from losing her head, the only thing that provided a link between what she had already experienced and what she was beginning to go through, was the bond between Laure and her, a bond both fresh and rotten, strong and tenuous, sophisticated and archaic, a cord from her body to Laure's, but which belonged to neither of them.

The Night of Withdrawal

'I hate heroin. I hate dope.'

It was night again.

Since coming back from holiday, Elsa had found her nights long, disrupted, important . . . very important. More important than usual. And yet it was dark as usual, outside and in. Occasionally in the distance a light burnt in a house like a beacon. The dark was at once empty and teeming with life; everything was the same. But for Elsa it wasn't the same any longer. Her life was pandemonium; her days unfolded with no end in sight; fatigue, sleep, and wakefulness didn't enter into it. She had lost all her habits; they no longer existed. For her, it was a time of birth and death, a time that could not be divided, could not be used up.

That night they had arrived in Hyères at a hotel Elsa knew.

During the three days she had waited in Paris, when she had contemplated Laure's abduction (the only way she could accept their departure was to think of it as an abduction: abducting her daughter from the madman and the others, from drugs), she had imagined that in this hotel everything would set itself right, because it was so beautiful.

59

The Hôtel de la Falaise was perched atop a cliff of red rock. At the foot of the cliff, small gardens nestled amongst the muddle of boulders, forming bowers of moss and horse-tail; many had a pond with water-lilies or tufts of papyrus in the middle. Rust-coloured paths ran across the cliff-face, zig-zagging down an easily negotiable, although somewhat steep slope. The inevitable, almost vertical drop to the sea was also covered with undergrowth: eucalyptus and sea pines sown there by the wind shot up out of the rubble. The straight trunks of the trees and the tangle of their branches made an open-work roof and formed what looked like a chaotic cloister giving onto land and sea. The smell of humus and seaweed filled the air. And the promise of bathing was repeated with each glimpse caught through trunks or rocks, each time one looked up, each time one's attention strayed from the steep path.

Bathing, swimming.

Laure would be reborn here, Elsa was certain.

She had anticipated that at this time of year the hotel would be empty or almost, and when they had arrived a few hours earlier, late in the afternoon, she had seen that she was right; they would be virtually alone here. Everything would turn out for the best.

During each lull that night, instead of resting, Elsa retravelled the road from Paris to the hotel again. She recalled all the stages of their journey, from the departure to this exact moment, as if her forty-two years of existence could be summed up in those few hours, as if she knew nothing else. At every pause, every time the attack seemed to be passing, she relived the trip – the stops, the conversations, the silences, the landscape – each time in greater detail; every particular was precious. She remembered how, as soon as they had taken their bags up to the room, she had led Laure down amongst the rocks and trees to the bottom, down to the calm, deep water; how Laure had shivered although it was warm; how instead of being lit up by the reddening light of the setting sun, her face had become paler; how instead of casting off her clothes and plunging in, she had huddled in her old jumper; how she, Elsa, had finally decided that all this behaviour was unacceptable, that it was simply evidence of Laure's ill temper, her capricious nature.

To prevent Laure from breaking a limb by knocking against something or falling, Elsa clasped her tightly, entwining her body in her daughter's. Laure's convulsions were so violent that the two of them were thrown off the bed, against the wall, across the mattress. Often Elsa couldn't hold on; often she would clutch at anything – an arm, a leg, a shoulder, a hip – but it would slip from her grasp, escape. The main thing was to keep Laure from hitting her head! Elsa was struggling in a torrent of suffering, in the savage stream of Laure's suffering. Later she would realise that they had been naked, that as they wrestled, their clothes had torn and they had wound up with nothing on, but at the time she paid no attention. What she had seen in the early evening, when the attack had begun, when Laure's long white smock had first torn and then shredded, was not her child's nakedness, but the hundreds of needle marks along the pathways of her veins. Dozens of red, pink, pinkish spots. Septic bites. Small circles of pus. Serous buds. Scabs. All over her arms, legs, inner thighs. The sight pierced Elsa's heart, brain, womb. She understood why Laure hadn't undressed in front of her, neither in Paris that first night, nor here earlier, to dive into the water. She had visions of accursed dolls stuck full of pins.

On the way back up from the beach, Laure had been in such a foul mood that Elsa had decided they would eat in their room. She ordered Parma ham and Châteauneuf du Pape, which Laure loved; something to put her in better spirits. But Laure scarcely touched a thing. She lifted a slice of ham on the end of her fork, nibbled a bit, then chewed it as if it were blotting paper. Elsa watched her and did mental sums: this was all costing a fortune, and she didn't like waste. Her mood changed then; she had had enough of this farce; her patience had run out. But she had chosen to say nothing rather than scold her daughter: 'This trip is costing me a packet. I'm sacrificing my whole life for you. You could at least eat or say thank you.'

She had said nothing.

They went to bed. Elsa put out her lamp and so did Laure. Elsa tried to calm down and go to sleep. She had driven nine hours on a motorway full of lorries; she was exhausted.

In the empty hotel, in the quiet of their room, every movement could be heard, the slightest sound. Laure couldn't stay still. In exasperation, Elsa said, 'Turn on the light and read. If you can't sleep, do something. Let me get some rest. I can't stand it any more.'

'I can't sleep.'

'All right then, let's talk. What's the matter with you, tossing and turning like that?'

'Give me a Tranxene.'

Elsa had forgotten about the Tranxene! She got up, rummaged through her handbag, went to get a glass of water, and handed Laure a little white pill, which she swallowed. Elsa sat on the edge of her daughter's bed and held her hand. She would talk to her until the Tranxene took effect. It wouldn't be long . . . Laure's hand was trembling like a mouse. It was as if her flesh were delirious; it was twitching with spasms and shocks. Elsa felt tremors coursing beneath the skin. Little by little she realised it wasn't just Laure's hand, but her arm, shoulder, torso – her entire body was like that. Her entire electrified body was quivering. Elsa had never seen anything like it.

'What's the matter, Laure? What's the matter?'

'I'm in withdrawal, it hurts!'

'What do you mean withdrawal? You said it was just the first twenty-four hours that were hard. You should be better, the hardest part is over with.'

'I had a fix.'

'When?'

'In the loo at the service station, when you bought petrol after lunch.'

'So the first day is just starting?'

Just as Laure said yes, there was a terrific noise, like an engine letting off steam; it was as if all the air in her body were being expelled. The hand Elsa was holding escaped; the arm shot straight up, smashing into the bedstead. Had she broken her arm?

'Are you all right?'

Instead of answering, Laure began to thrash about convulsively, kicking, crawling. Fear flashed across her face; she clenched her jaw until it seemed as if her teeth would break. Her eyes were eloquent, but she was unable to utter a word. And then she thrashed more and more, taking large, hysterical, useless swipes, striking furniture and objects, wreaking havoc.

Elsa thought her daughter must be having a epileptic fit. Was it an epileptic fit? She tried to pin down her legs and arms, but couldn't. At the same time she told herself that it wasn't epilepsy, that it was something similar but not that, since Laure was conscious of everything that was going on. But what else could it be? She grabbed her around the waist, immobilising her legs with her own, then hugged her upper body with all her strength.

'Where does it hurt, Laure?'

'Everywhere! You've no idea how much it hurts! Give me a Tranxene. Two, they told me two at a time! Now! Quick!'

Two little white pills. Watching Laure swallow them, Elsa thought they would be enough to knock out a horse, but they didn't seem to be having any effect on her wasted body.

For several months – close to a year, in fact – ever since she had begun to write her paper for the Sydney conference, Elsa had been haunted by her own ignorance. The deeper she went into her research, the more she realised just how vast her ignorance was. But she refused to think about it, telling herself she would fill the gaps, she would learn more. But the further ahead she got, the more ignorant she discovered others were – even the experts, those who knew. Initially she didn't want to admit it; she thought she was just being pretentious and lazy.

One day when she had been pestering Professor Greffier with a barrage of questions, he had said, 'Listen, the sun isn't in *our* system, we're in the solar system. We don't know how to capture all its energy. It's impossible to channel disorder into order – impossible.'

That night Elsa realised that what she knew would not help her control the energy driving Laure; it was impossible. The things she knew were useless. Suddenly, that night, she was no longer certain of anything except the suffering of her child. All her knowledge dissolved. What she knew about Tranxene, what she knew about the body, what she knew about psychology, epilepsy, will, disorder, madness – none of it was any use. It simply wasn't any use. She was up against something else, another life, and it was terrifying. All at once, the temptation to flee that had been with her often in the last few days vanished, because the ignorance in which she was foundering was there, was tangible; it existed, it was visible, it had to be confronted; nothing else mattered. The only certainty was Laure's incomprehensible suffering.

She had made herself fast to her daughter; her body followed the curve of Laure's exactly. Her mouth was right next to Laure's ear. She talked to her non-stop, softly. She didn't even know what she was saying; she murmured, mumbled; she was all Laure's.

'It's been almost an hour since you took the Tranxene. Is it helping at all?'

'No, not at all. I can feel it starting again. Pass me a couple more, please.'

Two more little white pills. She looked the length of the thin, naked body she was holding in her arms, at the thickness of the joints, the knees, the elbows, the bones protruding under the punctured skin, the torso – images of the charnel-house. Why isn't she out like a light? What did they teach me? What good was my training? Am I killing her?

Death was there, in the guise of Tranxene tablets. Laure asked for them and Else gave them to her. One, then two, then two more, and then . . . Elsa gave her the pills because she didn't know what else to do; they were all she had to offer. She needed an idea, a diagnosis, a plan for the future, but she had none. Elsa didn't understand what reality her daughter was going through, she just submitted to it. Laure's captive body led the dance. If Laure had asked for arsenic, Elsa would have given it to her. She actually would have given it to her! Realising the danger, but without making a conscious decision, Elsa rose and flushed the rest of the Tranxene down the toilet. She threw away her only weapon, and it gave her strength at a time when she thought she no longer had any. She went back to Laure and lay down beside her again. She took her in her arms and held her tightly, as she had done all night, whispering in her ear, 'I've just thrown away the Tranxene. I don't want to give you any more. I don't want to give you anything else. I don't want to kill you.'

There was a silence. It was as if the words had not penetrated Laure's consciousness. And yet she had heard them, Else was certain. And then suddenly she yelled, 'I don't give a damn about dying! I don't give a damn! I don't want to suffer any more, that's all I want. Don't you understand, Elsa?'

'I understand. But I don't want to give you any more pills without knowing.'

'Knowing what?'

'How far I can go with them, what the maximum dose is.'

'Maximum dose, maximum dose! Are you crazy? Do you realise what you've done? What's going to happen to me now? I need a tranquilliser, a really strong tranquilliser.'

'Tranxene 50 is strong, very strong, and you've taken a lot. Anyway, you're suffering less now. We can have a conversation, and an hour ago that was impossible. You're getting better.'

'You obviously don't know what I'm going through! I'm suffering. It hurts. It's atrocious! I need something. I absolutely must have something. Get me some morphine!'

'But Laure, I'm not a doctor. I can't get morphine just like that.'

'They know you – in Paris they give you whatever you want.'

'In Paris, in my own neighbourhood, because they know what I do and they know I'll bring them a prescription within twenty-four hours, but not here.'

'Go on. People have heard of you. People know who you are.'

'No, Laure, they don't know me here.'

'You don't want to help me!'

'If I didn't want to help you I wouldn't be here. But I can't keep giving you drugs without knowing what I'm doing.'

'Morphine's the only thing that will do me any good.'

65

Laure wasn't being dishonest, she wasn't lying, she wasn't putting on an act. Laure had two voices! She was possessed. Elsa understood what hooked meant. Now she knew what it was like to be hooked. It was diabolical! She thought she was listening to her daughter speak, when in reality it was the heroin she was hearing. Yes, that was it, it wasn't Laure speaking, it was the heroin that had taken over Laure's voice; it was the heroin that wanted morphine. And Elsa didn't know how to respond to heroin. All she knew about heroin was that having a conversation with it would do no good. It was mad! She no longer knew what to say.

'We can go to hospital.'

'No, no, not hospital. Never. Promise me you'll never put me in hospital. Promise! Anyway, I won't go.'

'Listen, Laure, if things go on like this, I don't see any other solution.'

'Never, never. I'm getting out of here!'

She jumped up and began rummaging in the shambles of the room, searching for her things. Everything was in disarray: sheets, pillows, blankets, clothes, the supper tray, the open suitcases. Furniture was out of place; a bedside lamp had been knocked over and its shade crushed. It struck Elsa now that the room was just as her flat was the day she arrived home. Laure thrashed about in the mess with incredible energy. She was naked, and her veins stood out like tattoos on her emaciated body, like the borders in a geography of torture. A map of hell. Again Elsa though of sacrificial dolls, of carnival skeletons.

'Listen, one of my old friends is a psychiatrist in Marseilles. I can call him. Or we can go to see my parents in Aix.'

She had been thinking about it all night. Who could help them? Who could come to their aid? Who could relieve her, if only for five minutes?

Laure stopped.

'OK, call your pal the shrink.'

Marseilles. All day a dusty heat had been blowing in through the open windows, along with the sound of car horns, voices, the aroma of *ratatouille*. The large Mediterranean city that Elsa knew so well was there, outside. And yet she had become a stranger to it. Every sound, every light, served only to accentuate the strange distance that separated her both from what she knew and from what she did not yet know.

A hundred times that day Elsa had thought they wouldn't make it. She had seen the time coming when she would have to take Laure to hospital by force. Her friend the psychiatrist was saying, 'On top of the Tranxene you gave her last night, I've given her a dose of tranquillisers usually reserved for severely manic patients. Ordinarily she'd be knocked out, you know, and yet it looks as if it hasn't had any effect on her.'

Laure prattled on, arguing constantly. She kept coming back to morphine, saying that only morphine would do anything for her. Elsa's friend discussed it with her: 'Laure, what you want is heroin. Please realise that. Even if you don't realise it, your body does and is demanding it. I don't want to sedate your body with morphine because it's an opiate just like heroin or methadone . . . That's the old-fashioned way. They used to get people off opium by putting them on morphine. They were no longer opium addicts, they were morphine addicts. Do you want to stop or not?'

'I want to stop, but morphine is nothing like heroin. I'd just have a little tiny hit and it would calm me down. You could watch me do it. I wouldn't be high, just calm, that's all.'

Now it was all over and Laure was asleep.

When she had finally understood she would not be getting any morphine, she had lain down and shut her eyes, defeated.

Elsa sat down beside her daughter, placed a hand on her

forehead, stroked her temples; she felt the spasms become further and further apart until they finally subsided. The upheaval was over.

Her friend had watched them for a long time and then gone off to take a shower.

She heard the water running and it did her good; it was like a storm breaking. Later she heard her friend go into the next room, where he turned on a lamp. A rectangle of light flooded through the open doorway to Elsa's feet. Her friend said nothing, didn't move, but she knew that he was listening attentively to what she was doing.

A very, very, very long time ago, as their childhood was drawing to a close, they had gone to the same *lycée* and had fallen in love. Or rather, enchanted, together they had discovered love. But then she had met Jacques . . .

Softly, certain he was listening, Elsa said, 'Life is strange, isn't it?'

The answer came right away, 'Yes . . . Is she asleep?'

'Yes, sound asleep. She's exhausted.'

'Come and talk, then.'

They talked about drugs, about Laure, about their work. They were experts. He knew about Elsa's work and admired her. He did most of the talking. Elsa watched him the whole time, watched his eyes, his hands, the way he sat in the armchair. Love was a memory between them, a buried treasure that couldn't be recovered, but it was a peaceful part of the past. It was restful.

As they spoke knowledgeably, their voices seemed to drone on in repetitious recitation, a performance, a lullaby. Again she felt like a stranger. She was too tired to keep up a serious conversation. She couldn't stay awake any longer; she went to lie down beside Laure.

She wasn't surprised the next morning to find herself where she was, to see Laure as she was, dazed with sleep. She knew they were in Marseilles. The images of the last few days had not left her during the night; they had mingled with her dreams.

On the floor beside her were books she had taken from her friend's bookcase last night, before going to lie down with Laure: books on the psyche, psychology, psychiatry, psychoanalysis. She looked at them, knowing she wouldn't open them: not now, not later, not tomorrow. She knew them by heart, with all her heart. She knew they couldn't help her any more; she had to get beyond them. She didn't know how she knew, she just knew. It was all very abstract.

She thought, *I am elsewhere, I am afterwards*; she was unable to think simply *I am*. She clung to 'elsewhere' and 'afterwards', but they slipped away because the essential part, *I am*, was missing. It was all very abstract. Heroin had abstracted Elsa. She was floating in a sea of vagueness; a mooring line had snapped and she was adrift. Elsa was being tossed by a wave, and she didn't know if she would find her footing again. It didn't worry her; that wasn't the important thing. The important thing was . . .

Elsa was a solitary person. She had not become one, she had always been like that.

Her parents were quiet, loving people. They ran a shop selling men's and women's undergarments in Aix en Provence. Business was brisk. They lived in the flat over the shop; Elsa was born there. It was a bright spot, peaceful and calm, in the centre of town. The bedrooms overlooked a garden where a plane tree stood, so tall that virtually nothing else could grow there; it took up all the room. In winter it lost its leaves. Then, as a child, Elsa could see the ground broken in places by the tree's grey-green roots, like half-buried snakes. She used to love all that and still did – the house, the shop, the plane tree, her father, her mother – but she didn't feel deprived of them, she didn't miss them. She saw her parents rarely; only on affectionate visits to celebrate some occasion. She wrote once a month. They telephoned each other if there was a birth or death, or an examination, or to organise holidays: simply to keep in touch, because they cared for each other. One day death would bring their relationship to an end. That was in the nature of things: her parents were old.

Laure's death would not be in the nature of things!

If Laure died during Elsa's lifetime, that would be chaos. Elsa had to be the one to endure it first, to blaze the trail. As for Laure's first steps: 'Don't be afraid, my arms are right here on the other side. Just one step, don't be afraid.' As for her birth: 'Don't be afraid, my thighs are right here on the other side. Don't be afraid, it's just one push.'

If only parents didn't die . . . But one couldn't survive the death of a child – it was unbearable, unthinkable!

Laure took drugs. Laure could die. Elsa knew that all it took was one fix too many . . . She also knew that Jacques was dead, that he knew the way . . . She was afraid of Jacques, of Jacques' judgment; she couldn't hand over her daughter in the state she was in. The idea had stowed away in a corner of her mind; it was unworthy, idiotic. She wanted nothing to do with it. She rejected it. She wore herself out rejecting it, but she couldn't put it behind her. She no longer knew how to think; all she could do was see images.

Only images, flashes, snapshots that motivated her or stopped her, childhood memories that came back to her.

Often she was in Aix, a little girl in her room. A bee, sated with linden, buzzed now and again. It was June, the end of the school year. She enjoyed studying, enjoyed the harmony between the books from which she learnt and the plane tree she saw through her open window. Outdoors and indoors, pages and leaves, walls and sky, did not exist, only knowledge, which encompassed everything. And then there was the distant sound of the bell tinkling below whenever a customer entered the shop. Knowledge would be less illuminating without the echo of the bell in the calm of a Thursday afternoon.

And then sometimes it was winter, and she was in the shop near the cash register, standing back. There were three ladies to be served. One was waiting, one was inspecting stockings that Elsa's mother was showing her, and another wanted a slip; her father was helping her. He was wearing his brown wool suit, his stiff-collared white shirt, and his black tie. It was raining outside. Water from the customers' umbrellas was pooling on the floor around the umbrella stand. Her father had a precise, expert way of showing off the trimmings. He cupped his hand and slid it into the top part of the slip as if it were a breast, opening his fingers to show how dainty and transparent the lace was. She didn't like it when he did that; she turned away and looked at her mother or the umbrellas or the street through the shop window.

And then it was later with Jacques, and she was in her early teens. He wanted to buy some rubbers and when the chemist asked him what brand and what size, he didn't know what to say. He went bright red and ran out of the shop as if it were on fire. Then the chemist, in a professional, indifferent way, gazed questioningly at Elsa: did she know the brand and size? Elsa said, 'We'll see,' and left as well, overcome with the giggles. Jacques, distraught, was waiting for her a little further along the street. 'I'm such an idiot.'

'It's all your fault. Why'd you want to buy rubbers anyway?'

'But what if we made a baby, Elsa!'

'We'd have a baby, like everyone else.'

She didn't mind the idea of having a baby. She knew she'd have one eventually.

Sometimes, when Elsa was a child at the beach, she would let the waves drag her off. Her parents would take her to Saintes Maries de la Mer, usually in June or September, for family picnics.

Often it was very windy and they had to lash down the beach umbrella so it wouldn't blow away. She once saw a strong gust rip it out of the ground and spin it along the beach like a Catherine wheel, so quickly that even her father, who could run quite fast, wasn't able to catch it. The umbrella ended its flight in the waves, which tossed it about awhile for their amusement.

On days like that the boom of the surf was so loud that Elsa couldn't hear her parents warning her to be careful. She knew that they were doing it, she saw them in the distance waving their arms to call her back, she saw their mouths opening wide, probably to shout 'Don't go too far!', 'Be careful!', 'Stay near the shore!', 'Come back!', but because of the thunder of the waves, she didn't hear the words. She couldn't hear them and, in any case, she didn't wish to hear them. Her ears were full of the crashing of the breakers as flow exploded into ebb. Her ears were full of the roar, and her nose, eyes, and skin full of salt spray and wind. The skin between her fingers and between her thighs, the skin of her neck, the skin of her back and buttocks, of her stomach, all her skin was shiny and whipped by the nor' wester and its din. The sun, straight overhead, open and large, let its warm gaze fall upon her. Not the tiniest cloud was to be seen in the sheer blue sky. The Mediterranean, made yellow and green by the sand and sediment it churned up and carried in its waves, was full of sharp grains that pricked Elsa's feet and legs as she waded out into the water. She couldn't resist the beauty of the roiling surf and wanted to play with it. Play, just play; not drown, not die. She knew she was taking a risk.

She had to go out a little further to play; the water had to be up to her calves, her knees, even her thighs. The bottom seemed constantly to be giving way under her. The sand, drawn out to sea by the retreating waves, slipped from under her feet, became fluid; her toes gripped nothing but water. She lost her balance. She stumbled. She continued to advance as well as she could, the beach liquidly sliding, until a breaking wave took advantage of her instability. Swept off her feet by the wave's circular motion, Elsa found herself rolling in the watery womb, in a spinning matrix rushing headlong towards explosion. She no longer knew which way was up and which way was down, what was sky and what was sea. Blinded, choking, she realised she had gone too far; she would never get out of this whirlpool. She no longer had any weight or dimensions, and it was threatening to drag her down into the bottomless depths of the sea. And then she felt a sudden jolt as her body struck *terra firma*. Just in time; she was breathless! And then she had to get back on her feet, resist the ebbing wave in which she had been lost. Otherwise the gaping maw of the next roller would swallow her. It was rushing in close; she had to face it . . .

The next morning in Marseilles, when she opened her eyes, Elsa remembered all that, the pleasure she had taken as a child in putting herself in danger.

Laure moved; she was on her back. Still asleep, she abruptly thrust one leg to the side in a bizarre way, hitting her mother, who had been daydreaming. Elsa suddenly became alert again, and the images in her head were thrown into disorder. Laure's body.

Drugs, the shadow of death, gave Elsa's past, all that she had experienced before drugs, symbolic significance. The past was over, she no longer learnt anything from it – as if her life had ceased. Henceforth, she would think in terms of 'before drugs' and 'after drugs'. Incidents from before began to stand out from what was still the uninterrupted flow of her existence; separate, each became significant in its own way, became a marker blazing the trail of her old knowledge, leading her to the enigma of Laure's body.

It's raining. I've missed the train to Paris. The next one is in fifty-five minutes. I'd rather stay here than go back to my parents' place. They'll tell me again that in the state I'm in, five months pregnant, or almost, I'd be better off living with them until I give birth. As if Jacques didn't exist! As if we weren't a couple! They do respect Jacques, but in their opinion, you don't expect a child in a maid's room in the thirteenth *arrondissement*. I don't like to hurt them but their attentiveness is unbearable.

Elsa bought a weekly paper, the kind that Jacques used to call a rag. That didn't stop her reading one sometimes anyway, on the quiet. There was no one in the waiting room. She sat down on a bench near a picture window from where she could see the deserted platform in the rain, a railcar on a distant track, and even further off, a lone carriage, water streaming down its sides, the stumps of its buffers ready to bump into nothingness, emptiness. She had always liked the weak uncertain light of train stations. Leaving. Arriving. Passing through.

She was passing through. A little over a year ago she had been living here in this city, in a street, in a house, in a room in this city; the rest of the world had been elsewhere and today here she was, passing through. It had happened quickly. Becoming an adult hadn't been hard. She had thought it would be more complicated. Little by little her parents would grow accustomed to the separation and it would be as simple for them as it was for Elsa. If only it turned out like that, if only they weren't unhappy. She loved them.

She stretched her legs, putting her feet up on the bench opposite, on the 'rag' she had put down so as not to soil it with her shoes. She would read the paper later. She gazed at the falling rain, the steel of the rails, the two seemingly infinite stiff parallel spines, and imagined their countless connections, the great networks of rails that took the trains to the warmth, to the cold, everywhere, through cities, deserts . . . and the thousands of rail buffers along the coasts, at the water's edge. The ports, the ships, the loading and unloading. She rested. Every cell in her body gave itself unreservedly to the life that was its own. Elsa was in complete harmony with herself. This state of abandon lasted a long time, until gently but distinctly a new sensation forced her to pull herself together. A light touch, a fleeting feeling, a small slide, a light, blue toboggan had crossed her middle, deep within her body. The child had moved! For the first time! She recognised it; no one else could move like that. The child was no longer an idea, a supposition, extra weight, a future. The child was living there inside Elsa. There was a body inside her body, a stranger in her midst, someone who moved while she rested. She was happy. Tears welled up in her eyes. She placed her hands on her belly, apprehensively, inquisitively, hopefully, tentatively . . . She scarcely dared touch her belly. Then nothing; the child stopped moving. Her child was resting, too. Again she looked out at the rain, but now there was another gaze within her gaze, other eyes within her eyes, another belly within her belly. Her child was passing through here, too, like her, with her.

She rose and went to the telephone box. She shut herself inside. She was extraordinarily joyful and serene. She called her parents. 'Hello, it's Elsa . . . Everything's fine, just fine, but my train's a little late, so I thought I'd phone to say goodbye again quickly. Well, bye then. I've got to go now or I'll miss the train.'

She hadn't said a thing. In the end she hadn't told her parents that the child had moved. She had waited until it moved a great deal before she told Jacques. She had waited until she couldn't hide it any longer.

Laure's body.

The mystery of the body, Laure's body. So many months passed in intimate physical contact without even seeing each other, with her knowing nothing more of me than my womb, with my knowing nothing more of her than the shape of her back in my hands, through my skin. No, to be honest, we did know a little bit more than that about each other; we knew something of each other's rhythms.

Laure's birth. My astonishment when I realised that my baby and my body had decided to put an end to it, that to them the time was ripe. They sought deliverance in a way that I rejected. I wanted to bring my child into the world at my own pace, not theirs, which took no account of my suffering. Their hysterical, paroxysmal pace!

'Relax, Madame Labbé. Don't tense up. Relax your thighs. This is it. Go on! Breathe in. Breathe out. Push! Push, push, push, push! Good, here it comes. I can see the head.'

He can see the head and I can't! Together, the doctor, the baby and my body are experiencing something that I didn't agree to, and yet it is happening in me and with me. Whether I like it or not, I am part of it. I can't even argue about it. I'm defeated . . .

'That's fine, Madame Labbé, you're relaxing. This should be the last one. Breathe in. Breathe out. Bear down! Push hard! Push, push, push . . . There it is . . . It's coming . . . Again, again, again . . . There it is! It's a girl! You have a little girl, Madame Labbé!'

The naughty little thing is on my belly. Wet, pink, bloody, down plastered to its skull. My little Laure. What a beauty. What a miracle.

Laure's body.

Laure's body when she dives.

Laure's body when she dances.

Laure's body when she's sitting at her desk.

Laure's body in front of the mirror, when she's getting ready to go out.

Laure's heroin-spangled body, a victim of deceitful happiness. Her youth streaming out through the holes in her transparent skin. And along the cord from her umbilicus to mine runs that bitch junk.

Elsa began a new life in which Laure's body alone bore witness to her knowledge.

There were signs; for example, a mole at the corner of her left eye. When Laure was three days old, Elsa had mistaken it for a speck of dust. Now it had grown to a flirtatious little beauty spot. Last night Elsa had noticed it as Laure spoke, demanding morphine, moving her emaciated and pustulated limbs, and because of the mole, Elsa, instead of seeing Laure as she had become, gesticulating before her, saw her tiny baby, her little girl, her child, her Laure. It had knotted her stomach . . . Saw the first joints of Laure's left hand, still slightly misshapen, from being crushed in a deck chair when she was four. Elsa couldn't see them without the light and smell of that day coming back to her immediately, the little girl in her arms, brave, in pain, but not wanting to cry, seeing her own pain in her mother's eyes and repeating, 'It's OK, don't be afraid.'

This child constantly appeared before her mother, deceiving her. Elsa continued to live in the present, loving a body that Laure herself had eliminated. It was no use. She had to stop being moved by this body that no longer existed. She had to forget her child and become attached instead to this strange woman, to the body this strange woman had made for herself, with its marks of heroin. That was hard. That was the hardest part.

Afterwards, Elsewhere

First there were the ten days in Marseilles when Laure went through physical withdrawal. Then they went to warm themselves in the Moroccan sun for two weeks. Laure often got the shivers; she was always chilled to the bone.

Two rough weeks near Agadir. A fortnight of ups and downs that followed Laure's shifting moods. One hour she would be fine, the next she would be ill; one hour she would have a vacant look in her eyes, the next she would be in a sort of trance; one hour she would be as miserable as could be, the next she would laugh at everything; one hour nothing would appeal to her, the next she would absolutely have to have the most ridiculous things. When Elsa tried to find the thread that ran through all her moods, she couldn't. She questioned Laure and Laure began to cry. She became irritated: Why was Elsa asking all these questions? Laure couldn't understand her own behaviour and her helplessness exasperated her. She tried to defend herself but was intelligent enough to know that her explanations were worthless, and so she blamed her mother and made threats. Threatened to kill herself, threatened to get hold of some heroin in the next five minutes: 'It's everywhere, you know. The day we arrived here I could've told you where I'd find some, who'd have got some for me!' Elsa knew it was true; she stopped asking questions.

All she had to do all day was follow Laure's moods. She had never lived like that before, in a state of idle preparedness. She guessed her daughter's bizarre behaviour was not the result of caprice or a neurotic condition, but of mysterious urges created by heroin; Laure herself was unaware of them, but still she struggled with them. It was an absurd, pathetic struggle. Elsa became the spectator to the fight, the witness: she was there, that was her role. She was simply there, but she was always available and Laure knew it.

It was in Morocco that Elsa got into the habit, whenever Laure scandalised or worried her the most, of giving herself over to the contemplation of insignificant facts, trivia. One day towards the end of their stay, Laure went riding on the beach with a gang of young louts. They had rented her a worn-out old nag for a ridiculous price. Laure knew they were asking an astronomical sum, but she absolutely had to ride the animal, whatever the cost. Elsa had given in, had given her the money. She had seen Laure half naked – her body still covered by a constellation of pink dots that could by then pass for insect bites – galloping dangerously among the bathers; she had seen her gazing provocatively at the louts, she had seen her terrorising children building sand castles; she had seen their parents insulting her, shaking their fists at her. During the cavalcade, the people next to her on the beach had turned to look at her, knowing that Laure was her daughter, to prompt her to intervene. They had seen Laure scheming to obtain the money for the horse; they had seen her negotiating with the group of rough boys, her comings and goings between them and her mother. They looked at her with the disgusted expression that adults put on when confronted with irresponsible parents. Elsa had let them; she knew she couldn't stop the shameless display. Why was Laure, who was usually so proud, doing it? Why was Laure, who was by nature so scrupulous, making such a spectacle of herself? Rather than speak the unacceptable truth, rather than betray Laure, rather than complain, Elsa preferred to shut her eyes and offer her pale skin up to the sun. She decided to take an interest solely in the difficult relationship between her skin and the sun. But she had chased from her mind whatever she knew about ultraviolet rays and the epidermis: her failure with Laure made her fear all knowledge. So she said nothing, either to the people next to her or to her daughter. If Laure wanted to discuss her behaviour afterwards, they would discuss it.

She could not stand the person that Laure had become, yet at the same time she loved her more than she loved herself.

When they returned to Paris, which was reddening in autumn, the first relapse occurred.

Elsa had been convinced that the worst was over with, that now she would be able to get back on her feet and take care of rescuing Laure once and for all.

As soon as she arrived home, she called her friend in Marseilles to tell him about their two weeks in Morocco. He advised getting Laure to expand her circle of acquaintances. He said, 'She's too isolated. She needs to see people from her world who are not dangerous to her, ex-drug addicts . . . Sort of to do what they do in Alcoholics Anonymous. They help each other a lot. It works.' Laure took the phone, and they talked. In the end Laure said she knew a guy named Alex who had tried heroin but had quit.

Half an hour later Alex was there, charming, in good health.

Laure was smiling; she was pleased to see him and Elsa left them alone.

She went into her office to call Jacqueline. She, too, was pleased to talk to a friend again, to discuss business, to learn what had happened while she had been away. She chatted. She listened to her secretary, who had lots of questions for her.

Then Elsa heard someone go into the lavatory opposite – it must have been Laure because the door wasn't closed – and, a short time later, the sound of some metal object falling. The sound terrified her. She hung up right away, barely excusing herself.

From the doorway of her office, she could see Laure collapsed on the toilet, her shoulders sagging, her arms dangling, her left sleeve rolled up, in her right hand a cord and a syringe, and a teaspoon on the floor. Laure made what looked to Elsa like a considerable effort to lift her head. She had a faraway look in her eyes; she was smiling, she seemed gentle, she looked calm and satisfied, like a sleepy child about to be put to bed after supper, like someone who felt perfectly safe.

Laure's body was back! Her baby, her little baby!

Elsa crossed the corridor, picking her daughter up under the shoulders and knees.

She was heavy; how quickly children grow.

She carried her into her bedroom, laid her on the bed, and covered her up, though it was hardly necessary; Laure was warm as a little bird.

My baby, my little one, my darling . . .

'Did Alex give it to you?'

'Yes. I didn't want any, but it was just a little, just a tiny little bit.'

She slept.

For three weeks, Elsa had been watching Laure struggle with heroin, fight for heroin and against heroin, but she had never seen her give in to heroin. It was the first time that she had seen her daughter in bed with the white stuff. She found it indecent. She found it beautiful. This satisfied woman was Laure! She was ashamed of being there; she felt like a voyeur, she felt jealous . . .

My child, my child, what have they done to you!

Laure's body.

The peace she had felt the last few days in Morocco was gone. The peace of exile, of alienation, of solitude had been restful, reassuring – I don't know anything, I don't know anything or anyone.

Laure's inert body, the enchantment she saw on her daughter's impassive face, caused extremely intense emotions over which she had no control to well up in her. She was submerged by a primitive force that burst forth, whipping her, harassing her, slashing her. She no longer knew where she was or who she was. Her instinct was to keep on rocking Laure, on and on, mechanically. She waited for her heartbeat to slow, and then she rose.

On her way to the sitting room she kept herself agitated by taking large energetic strides that made her hold herself erect, made her taller. She thought of the Statue of Liberty, which she had seen close to at the entrance to New York harbour when she had sailed across the Atlantic once; a tall mature woman, big and strong, holding a torch aloft in her right hand. Elsa strode. The statue was striding with her; there was no doubt about it. But Elsa was going to use her torch to strike Alex in the face with all her might. That was certain.

She had never waged war, she had never fought, but that wasn't important. She didn't even think about it. She was going to give dear Alex a good thrashing, and that was all there was to it. No one could tell her that it was pointless, irresponsible. She couldn't care less; she would be responsible later.

He was expecting Laure to return, but instead he saw her mother striding towards him. He stared wide-eyed, drew back. Elsa gave him a terrific kick in the shins and it hurt.

'What are you doing? Cut it out!'

'Get out of here! Get out of my house, or I'll kill you!'

He whined as he rubbed his shins: 'She didn't pay me. I want to be paid.'

'You've got another think coming! You shouldn't have given her any drugs!'

'She's the one who rang me. She's the one who asked for it.'

'That's not true, you're lying. I was there when she called you. She didn't ask you for anything.'

He took refuge behind the settee.

'Listen, try to understand. She's a junkie and I'm a dealer. When a junkie phones a dealer and says she'd like to see him, you don't have to be a psychic to know what it means! You don't have to be a psychologist . . .'

He began to laugh. She hated him.

Hatred! Hatred was a Florentine cypress, tall, dark, pointed, slim. It towered over the welter of feelings. It was not debatable; there was no way to begin even to discuss it.

For three weeks Elsa had hated heroin – powder, dust, poison – but that evening she hated Alex, a human being. She could easily have slit his carotid and watched the blood gush out; it wouldn't have bothered her in the slightest.

She didn't know how to act with her hatred; she didn't know it well enough. That surprised her. She stopped.

The moulting period is a dangerous time. The creature must grow accustomed to a new state before trusting it fully. And then, while the creature is still moulting, still partly in its old state, and its new one is still too new to be livable, there is a time of great insecurity, great fragility to get through. Elsa was in a state of subtle change, paralysed by the intensity of her new feelings, and it frightened her. She knew that at any moment in this transitional state she could commit murder. She was in danger. So was Alex.

She really felt capable of killing Alex. If she had had a razor to hand, she would have slit his throat and taken pleasure in watching the blood spurt out with each beat of his heart, in geysers of gradually diminishing strength, until he hadn't a drop left.

If not for Laure at the other end of the flat, soft as an overripe fruit, rotten with drugs, she would have killed Alex. But Laure was there.

'Get out!'

'Pay me first.'

'How much?'

'Oh, it was just a tiny little fix . . . Two hundred francs. What a fuss for two hundred francs. She'll be down again in an hour.'

Elsa went to look for her handbag. She'd forgotten where she'd put it. She trembled with the effort of keeping her hatred in check. She found her bag and rummaged through it, no longer knowing what she was looking for. She felt as if there were twenty horses snorting inside her, moving, straining to get out. She kept muttering, 'It's my energy, it's my energy,' and it seemed to frighten her.

At last she remembered: she was looking for two hundred-franc notes. She returned to the sitting room, crumpling the notes in her fist. Alex was rifling through a drawer and in one of his hands he held a small female figurine of which Elsa was very fond. Made of painted ivory, it was old and pretty, an heirloom that had been in the family as far back as she could remember; her mother had given it to her not very long ago.

'What are you doing?'

'Nothing, just looking. I've never been here before.'

'And what's that in your hand?'

'This? Oh, nothing.'

He wasn't embarrassed; he put the statuette down. He smiled and was charming.

'Why do you do it?'

'Do what?'

'Sell drugs.'

'To pay my expenses!'

'What about your parents? Do they know?'

'My mum's dead.'

'How long ago did she die?'

'When I was six.'

'And your father?'

'My father? He goes through dustbins. My father doesn't notice a thing. My father's deaf; soon they're going to have to transplant dog ears on him!'

He burst out laughing. Raising an index finger on either side of his head, he flicked them up and down. He was rather funny.

'Why don't you try to quit?'

'What for? Some people drink, some smoke, some do winter sports – I do drugs, it's no big deal.'

Her hatred had crumbled; Elsa felt it giving way in her. In its place a weak indolent feeling set in: lassitude, disgust.

'Oh, get lost. I never want to see you again.'

Alex didn't need to be told twice. He took his money and left surprisingly quickly. 'A real little thief,' Elsa thought.

What calm! What emptiness! What confusion!

Alex had been frightened of Elsa's hostility, but he hadn't been frightened of Elsa. He had mocked her: 'You don't have to be a psychologist . . .'

This summer François had said a hundred times, 'Listen, baby, since the Sydney conference you've been at the top of your career.'

Elsa's research had produced some remarkable results. It wasn't actually very complicated. Of course she had worked, but then she liked working. Of course she had never let herself be distracted from her work, but then nothing distracted her better than her work. Of course her research was original, but then she didn't feel she was like other people. Of course her paper at Sydney respected tradition despite its originality, but then she didn't like a fuss. So . . . She hadn't done anything extraordinary and she had been the first to be surprised at the amount of interest her work aroused.

After Alex left, she settled firmly in the armchair, her arms on its arms, both feet flat on the carpet, slightly apart. She was in the position to be judged. She was in the dock.

She put herself on trial; she passed judgment on herself: 'I am useless. Elsa Labbé is useless. She can't even help her daughter.'

She went over her life since her 'triumph' at Sydney.

The general theme of the conference was 'Children's Imagination in the Late Twentieth Century'. Psychiatrists, psychologists, sociologists, psycho-sociologists, criminologists, and educationists would be there, even artists, including some whose names were highly respected. Elsa had been invited because of a paper she had published three years earlier on the drawings of pre-school children. The paper was based on her observations and reflections on the drawings of children she had had as patients over a fifteen-year period. It had created quite a stir in the scientific community when it had appeared. The invitation to Australia had in some ways been her crowning achievement and she had worked very hard preparing for the conference.

Elsa moved in the armchair. She though of Laure, in her room, stupefied by heroin. She lowered her head; her eyes were burning. She thought of what Laure had been doing while she was working on her paper . . . The visits Laure had made during that period . . . Nothing had happened.

'You're looking peaky, Laure.'

'Elsa, please, don't go all maternal on me.'

Her work, her research, her 'discoveries' – all, stemmed from a memory.

As a child she hadn't liked playing with dolls, but since she was a little girl she was given them anyway. She was only interested in her dolls on rainy days, boring days, days when she couldn't go out, when her parents were busy in the shop, when she had finished her homework and learnt her lessons, when she had tried to amuse herself every other way possible. Then, as a last resort, in late afternoon, almost evening, she would get her dolls and practise surgery on them. She would operate on little girls having appendicitis attacks. She would undress the doll and, using a pencil as a scalpel, begin to trace precise lines where she supposed that it hurt. And inevitably a moment would arrive when the point of the pencil would skid along the hard round stomach of the plastic doll and the line would get lost in the indistinct zone that dolls have between their legs. A narrow, flat, desert valley where the noisy, delicate leg joints met; a place condemned to irreparable amputations and crippling accidents. The surgeon would then take a pencil of another colour and start again. Once more the scalpel would skid. Elsa would become annoyed and in the end would scribble madly in circles, pressing with all her might on the tips, which often broke. She would be hot and sweaty, and could feel the blood rushing to her cheeks and ears. She had to pee but held it in, so she felt a pang in her stomach. She liked to get carried away by this mixture of haste and attentiveness. The bodies of her dolls were covered with scribbles that she concealed.

She would conceal them because they were private, not because she was ashamed. On certain important occasions she would give them a wash: on Christmas Eve, or the day before her birthday. The dolls would undergo great baths, great ablutions, in the bright daylight of the bathroom. Once, as her mother watched her, she said:

'Well, you do have funny way with your little girls. You're a little rascal, aren't you!'

They had laughed together. They knew why they were laughing and yet neither one of them would have been able to explain it. Later Elsa often thought about how it might have affected her sexuality if her mother had scolded her instead of laughing . . .

She heard the lift going up and down inside the building, its doors opening and closing automatically with a sigh. Sometimes there were voices in the corridors, muted and far off. People were coming home. Soon there would be the smells of soup, and the themes of evening television programmes would drift through the walls. It was the time when babies cry, children grow irritable, mothers become agitated and fathers are tired. The posh building couldn't smother all that completely.

Elsa sat in her armchair, caught in the trap of her own judgment. Laure lay on the bed as if dead, pale and motionless.

The first child she had had as a patient had refused to speak, although he was able. He was physically capable; he had no brain lesion, no throat lesion, no lesion of the vocal cords, lungs, or tongue . . . nothing to prevent him from speaking. He was a little over four years old. He had developed a simple but very clear language that had no articulated sounds. His name was Alain.

He was a placid child who went into a semi-prostrate state if Elsa became too curious. He couldn't stand intimacy; he wouldn't admit anyone into his universe. He did only what was absolutely necessary to survive; everything else happened completely within himself. He understood everything. You could tell he was capable of expressing anything, but he refused to communicate, except by making the odd grunt. He was timid, and he blocked out Elsa's life more effectively than a reinforced concrete wall, because she wanted to free him and couldn't.

Alain's mother was a charwoman. She would leave him at the clinic and come back to fetch him two or sometimes three hours later.

It was scrawls or doodling that enabled Elsa to crack the child's muteness.

Often when Alain was left to himself, he would edge quietly along the walls. Staring off into space, one shoulder against the wall, he scarcely moved, but did nothing else.

It was winter time. The electric lights were always on in the office, which she used only in the afternoon.

One day when she came in the morning and sunlight filled the room, she discovered a line, an irregular mark traced along the walls, about fifty centimetres from the floor. At first she simply saw it, but took no notice; then she became intrigued and started to examine it.

Looking closely, she saw that there were very light lines of different colours. 'Alain! Alain did this.' She was sure of it. She inspected the lines: there was nothing special about them; they were very light, and went up and down a little here or there and were occasionally broken probably because of the way he moved. In itself, each line was nothing unusual, nothing but the mark of a pencil dragged by a small hand. But they were proof enough that Alain had understood how a pencil could be used, that he could use it to mark his presence, to express his own existence. Did he do it every time he came or only sometimes? She erased a few centimetres of the lines in several places. Alain was coming the next day, and she would soon see.

The next day she watched him. As usual, while she wasn't working with him, he began his slow progress along the walls. Once she was alone at the end of the day, she saw that he had followed the same path. And each time he came he did the same thing. Did he always go in the same direction? No, sometimes he'd go one way, sometimes the other. Was the colour important? She purposely left only certain pencils lying about. No, the colour didn't matter; he used any pencil regardless of whether it was black or coloured. And if there were no pencil? She put all the pencils away in a drawer, leaving out only those she needed for the child with whom she was working. This time Alain started by ferreting everywhere until he finally decided to take the pencil of the little boy who had come after him. Elsa offered him hers, which, he refused. He insisted on having the other little boy's pencil, making him cry. It was the child's pencil that Alain wanted, not Elsa's. Finally she gave him a pencil and paper. She watched him out of the corner of her eye as he drew a few lines on the sheet of paper she had given him, and then began his snail's pace walk along the walls of the room again.

That very evening she inspected the entire length of every line, centimetre by centimetre. She discovered that once he reached the door frame – regardless of which side he approached it from – once he reached the hollow, in the deep angle formed by the wooden upright and the wall, he scribbled with all his might until the lead broke, or until the pencil skidded. Skidded! Yes, skidded . . . Just as it had with her dolls. Elsa saw herself scribbling frantically in the crotch of her dolls. It was something like that. That was what bothered Alain: the door. The pencil rarely skidded on the light paint of the wall; it skidded more on the dark wooden door frame. That was why she had never seen the marks before; they had to be right under your nose; they were well concealed. There were hundreds of them.

Was it the hollow? Was it the door? Was it the wood? Was it what lay beyond the door? Was it a noise?

First she realised that Alain was ambidextrous, since he always stood sideways when he reached the door, whether he had begun drawing from the left or the right. Once there, staring into space, he scribbled with the hand that was against the wall and hid the pencil. She noticed that these scribbles were no darker or defter on one side than the other. Then, during their sessions, she purposely tried to get Alain to use his left hand and soon found out that he could use either hand equally well. Beyond that nothing changed in the little boy's behaviour. But it was progress all the same. She spoke to his mother about it.

'Have you noticed that Alain is ambidextrous? He can use his left hand just as well as his right.'

'No, I hadn't realised. Ain't nobody like that in our family. Wouldn't mind being able to use both hands myself – things'd get done faster. Well, I'll tell my husband. He'll be pleased. He never says as much, but it worries him to see the boy like this.'

But Alain had still not said a word.

The door! The damned door! Elsa told herself that she was off on the wrong track, that she shouldn't get hung up on the door. She observed Alain secretly and when she saw him stop near the door and become absorbed in his scribbling, always standing sideways, as if nothing were happening, she tried to catch his eye. But he didn't look at her; he didn't look at anything.

Months passed. Elsa knew that at the end of the year she would have to write up a report. What could she say? Alain was now five. Next year he would be declared ineducable and classified as 'mentally retarded'. Perhaps next year, given the ineffectiveness of the sessions at the clinic, he would even be taken away from her and sent to a specialised institution. She became obsessed with Alain. Often she let her attention wander from other children to observe him. This couldn't go on much longer.

One beautiful Friday in early summer, Elsa was tired and longing for the day to be over. Alain was standing by the door, transfixed, like a dog pointing. Elsa could bear the sight no longer. So, contrary to everything she had been taught, contrary to the most basic rules of therapy, she took a drastic step. From where she was at the other end of the room, in a very dry authoritarian tone, she said: 'Alain! It's a door. Alain, say "door"!'

The child, surprised, clung to the wall and stared at her. In his eyes was a distress that overwhelmed Elsa. Tears welled in her eyes, and spilled over; the child saw them. Nothing else happened. Elsa finished the day distraught. She had made a serious professional error. Perhaps she had compromised the child's future forever. She no longer dared look at him. She felt as if she had spoilt everything. She blamed herself; all that nonsense about scribbling, what idiocy!

Alain's mother came to fetch him as Elsa was putting away her things. The woman took her son by the hand and, as she did each time, said: 'Say goodbye to Madame Labbé, Alain.'

Elsa didn't want to look. She knew Alain was going to wave goodbye like a ten-month-old baby. She didn't want to see that any more. Without lifting her head, she said, 'Goodbye, Alain. Goodbye, Madame.' Then she distinctly heard 'Door.' Very clearly articulated. And then again 'Door!' Alain was staring at her, his eyes wide with the effort he'd just made. In them was a questioning look, as if to say, 'Is that it? Are you happy?' Elsa came towards him and took him in her arms, not daring to hug him too tight. Holding back her tears, afraid that her emotional state might frighten him, she said, 'You spoke, you said "door". I'm very pleased. You can do it. You're a big boy. That's wonderful. Say it again for us, Alain. Say "door".'

He said, 'Door.'

Elsa said, 'The door.'

Alain repeated, 'The door.'

His mother said, 'He said something. He said "door".'

Elsa said, 'He even said "the door".'

His mother said, 'Dear God. Madame Labbé, it's a miracle! You've managed a miracle.'

They sat down to get over their emotions. Elsa held Alain while his mother spoke. Little by little she learnt the story of the closed door. It had started when Alain was a baby. He had been noisy, and at suppertime he made such a racket with his spoon that no one could hear anything. His father was tired and couldn't stand the din. It put him in a bad mood, so his mother had to take Alain in her arms to calm him and feed him that way. She couldn't even sit down. Her husband didn't like that either. That's why she decided to feed the little boy separately before his father got home.

'When the baby saw he wouldn't be eating with us, how he cried, Madame Labbé! He bawled fit to bring the roof down. We couldn't stand it, so we decided to put him in his room. He screamed! We shut the door. He screamed for a few more days and then calmed down. That's it, that's the whole story.

When he started to stand up, a little while later, he opened the door. It's just got a latch, not a knob. It's not hard to open. One day I thought he might've opened it, and when I went to check, I found that he'd managed to climb up onto the ledge of the window in the corridor. It was summer and we'd left it open. It was a close shave. He was almost out the window. I arrived just in the nick of time. What a fright it gave me! So I started locking the door and got into the habit. Who knows what goes on in his head? You never can tell with him. When he's in his room he can't hurt himself. That way I don't need a baby sitter . . . And since they don't want him at the nursery . . .'

'You could try opening the door. And leave him here with me while you're working.'

'Well, sure, if that's all. If you think it might help.'

'Let's give it a try.'

A month later Alain was talking, talking well. In his file Elsa wrote 'educable'.

Elsa never drew up a special report on Alain's case: her methods hadn't been very orthodox and she didn't want to boast.

Elsa Labbé was an educated person, better educated than most. She had become a specialist. She had stored up knowledge that helped her interpret psychological tests, even to develop her own, determine mental age, evaluate intelligence quotients . . . but she had learnt more than that. She had moved in a scientific universe that questioned itself. She had an insatiable desire to find out what surprises knowledge had in store for her. She felt well equipped to face those surprises.

Elsa's world had been the same from the day she was born. It had evolved, but it was no different. Her world was that of her parents: the world of France for the last century. She knew that it had not always been like that, that she could name and date stages in its development. She knew the excesses of the Enlightenment and where it had gone astray. She was aware of what had been gained and what had been lost. It all balanced out; there was an equilibrium. That world was worth whatever it was worth, was whatever it was; she criticised it, but felt part of it; it was her world and she loved it.

She loved it.

It was her era, her time, her part of history. She imagined how her life would unfold, knowing full well that she would have to make choices. She imagined those future choices and rejoiced in them: each choice meant a step forward.

And now Laure's history was colliding fiercely with her own, pulverising it. She was in pieces, she knew it. Under these conditions, how could she give her daughter any support when she herself had lost her underpinnings?

Elsa made this assessment as the memory of little Alain left her. She looked around; she was at home, but that didn't mean anything any more. At home, in herself, within herself – she now found it all extremely suspect.

She told herself that she had to conserve her energy if she wanted to hold out. She had to avoid planning, she had to stop organising the future and start responding as simply as possible to the present. No analysis, no lectures on morals, no solutions – or else basic solutions, solutions to preserve her daughter's health and her own for the time being, no more.

Laure had entered the sitting room without making a sound. She saw her mother upright in the armchair, staring into space. She had no idea how helpless Elsa was. How could she? She had never known her mother any other way but using her strength. She didn't know that Elsa's strength was derived from what she had learnt. She didn't know that in the last few weeks, Elsa's knowledge had served only to highlight her ignorance. She didn't know that her mother was a river run dry.

She approached her mother, who finally noticed her standing there and turned to gaze at her. The look of a little girl who'd made a mistake and was pretending to be very sorry came over Laure's face, and she slid onto Elsa's lap with a gentle, supple movement, slipping her arms around her mother's neck and shoulders, giving her a hug. She wanted to be rocked, to be cuddled; she was still basking in the junk's warmth. Elsa rocked her: not to forgive or console her, but because it did her good to rock; the light rocking rhythm soothed her. They rocked together until they had had enough.

Elsa said, 'Let's get something to eat.'

They went into the kitchen. Elsa opened the refrigerator and cupboards, hoping that an idea might suggest itself. Laure sat at the table, still dazed.

'How about an omelette with herbs, runny the way we both like it. Ham, salad, cheese, a glass of red wine, and some fruit. How does that sound?'

'Fine. Elsa, I can't stay in Paris. I know I won't be able to hold out.'

'All right then, we'll eat and then leave. OK?'

'OK. You're fantastic. What about your work?'

'I've taken care of it. Don't worry. Do you want to talk about it?'

'No. I'm all mixed up.'

Wandering became a way of life for them. There were a lot of relapses, bitter failures that cut both Elsa and Laure to the quick. Laure would be unable to hold out, unable to get over her craving for heroin, so they would leave again. There was never any question of reconsidering the agreement they had made the first day.

Wandering here and there; moving around the country. They fled Paris and people. Now they knew how to avoid the worst part of withdrawal. They had remedies. Elsa's friend the psychiatrist had given them prescriptions.

But there was no remedy for the other kind of withdrawal, the kind that came afterwards. The worst kind, the kind that destroyed desire, tortured desire, broke the spirit with its contradictory obsessions. It took Elsa a long time, a very long time, to learn about that kind of withdrawal, the kind Laure called 'psychological withdrawal'.

At the same time as she and Laure began to wander about together, psychological withdrawal sent Elsa's mind wandering along dizzying paths. From that point on, her knowledge would be like quicksand, her intelligence would be of no help, and she would lose her ability to communicate with other people.

End of the one hundred and forty-three pages

PART TWO

The following Monday she received me courteously, as usual. She told me that she was pleased with what I had written; that she found her own rhythms in it, her own vocabulary; that I had understood a great deal about her – her verbal tics, her obsessions – and that my style was well suited to the subject. She seemed genuinely satisfied and yet I found her more reserved, more wary than before.

I'd been afraid that I might have gone too far, been too crude at times. 'No, no. The world of drug addicts is like that, and I tend to be blunt myself, as you must have realised. Some days I let myself get carried away . . . Reading it the way you've rendered it made me relive that period and remember other traumatic incidents, other times of distress.'

We set to work again. I felt that something was holding her back. Often she was quiet; we spent long moments of silence together. She was making an obvious effort not to close up; she went over certain events we had already covered, especially the night of withdrawal. We returned to that passage, changing words here and there; we moved commas around. It seemed to her that there were no words to express her daughter's suffering. One day she began to cry, repeating, 'It's dreadful, it's dreadful. You can't imagine how they suffer. It's dreadful.'

The woman was falling apart before my very eyes. I was deeply shocked. I had always thought of her as being very self-possessed. I hadn't realised that the vertigo, the abyss she had often spoken of, was still there inside her. She had concealed something, or someone, from me. She was being hunted. But by whom? By what? Suddenly all I could see was her fragility, and I needed to get to know and write about that fragility. So I pushed, I pushed too hard.

I had just arrived one morning when she said, 'That's it, I have nothing more to tell.'

'That's impossible. We haven't got beyond anecdotes. Try to understand what I'm saying. It's now, at page 144, that we have to start talking not only about the end of Laure's story, but also about the background.'

'What background?'

'What you're always hinting at.'

'What am I hinting at?'

'I don't know . . . perhaps the vanity of "experts", the ignorance of "scientists" . . .'

'Oh, come now! You're letting your imagination get the better of you.'

'In any case, we haven't got enough for a book yet.'

'I never said I wanted to write a book. I never said that.'

'You're being dishonest.'

'OK, let's say I am. I just don't want to talk about it any more. You can't publish anything without my authorisation, anyway.'

'What do you mean, "Let's say I am"! I can't accept that. I want to continue.'

'All right then, do it by yourself. Say it took Laure three years to kick the habit and that will be that.'

'No, I won't do that. I don't know how she did it. I'm not going to make it up. The story would lose its authenticity. I haven't done all this work for that, for nothing.'

'I've paid you. You've had a cheque for ten thousand francs.'

'That's not what I mean. I mean that my work is supposed to lead to a book. There's a book there and I'm not going to let it drop. One of my friends died of an overdose a few months ago. I had stopped seeing her the last while. I couldn't stand the fact that she wasn't trying to quit. I was scornful of drug addicts. I didn't understand. She wrote poems . . . I felt that by helping you write your book I was making amends, that it might open other people's eyes. And then, I've become attached to the story; I've become attached to you. I want to see it through to the end.'

'But I have nothing more to say.'

'That's impossible. If you don't feel capable of talking

about the background, about what crushed you – because I know that something, or someone, did crush you – at least tell me the end of Laure's story.'

'Well, after three years my daughter finally stopped . . . I am moved by what you said about your friend who died, and the fact that it might help people see drug addicts differently . . . But all kinds of stories have been written about drug addicts. The facts are not the most important thing. The facts are terrible, but there are worse things. Drugs reveal a lot . . . There's something else, but I don't know what. It would be much too private. We wouldn't get anywhere with it, and I don't want to risk jeopardising my daughter's future. Ex-drug addicts are not highly thought of.'

'Well, that's easy. All you have to do is change the names and occupations.'

'Not my occupation. Otherwise it wouldn't make any sense.'

I changed the names and her daughter's occupation, but that didn't change her attitude.

'What if you finished the book by talking to a woman? There are all kinds of women who do the same thing I do and who are just as good. You might feel more comfortable.'

'No, I like the fact that you're a man, and young. You're not the obstacle, it's me. The obstacle's in me, but I don't quite know what it is.'

I continued to see her. Instead of talking to me about herself, she talked about moving. She was leaving her large place for a two-room flat.

She had given up her practice; I didn't think she had any money left. I wanted to clear up those two points. About work she told me, 'I don't dare tackle other people's unconscious any more.' And about money, 'I have no more money. I can't pay you any more than I already have.' I reassured her. If we managed to finish the book, I would accept a percentage of sales. She wouldn't be doing me a favour; that was standard.

I felt that she was on her guard, unsettled. She was waiting;

she wanted to talk about something other than moving, but she didn't.

Handling objects and clothing and papers accumulated over the years brought back memories. She told me about herself: her youth, her childhood, her daughter's childhood, her parents, their shop, Aix. I knew all that; it was already in the one hundred and forty-three pages. She knew that I knew, but she pretended to be scatter-brained: 'I'm so absent-minded. You have no idea how absent-minded I am.'

She was lonely. I wondered whether Laure was still alive, whether she might not be dead, whether that might not be what she was hiding. I even thought she might have invented her. Some days I suspected her of having invented the whole story. But on the day she moved, I saw Laure, a very beautiful young woman, very cheerful, very efficient. I thought of my dead friend, of what she had been like before getting into drugs. I thought she would have been able to stop, too, if I hadn't been such a fool . . . There was obviously a very close bond between mother and daughter; they were almost like lovers. But Laure didn't realise what her mother was going through, and Elsa did everything she could to hide it from her. That day she laughed, joked, and acted as if I were her boyfriend. I didn't dare speak to Laure. I was on Elsa's side and I couldn't betray her.

Laure was working outside of Paris then; she had come back just to help Elsa move and took the evening train home. After kissing her mother goodbye she said to me, 'Take care of her. She works too hard. I don't think she's looking well.' She didn't know that Elsa wasn't seeing patients any more. I wondered what kinds of stories Elsa had told her to justify moving.

Something very strong bound me to Elsa now. I couldn't define my feelings exactly. The memory of my dead friend entered into it, but that was more of an excuse than anything else. I wasn't in love with Elsa; I loved her. I loved her as if she were my daughter or my sister, not the way I'd loved other women. I went to see her every day.

After she moved into the small flat, she talked less and less. The entire month of February and part of March came and went without her saying much more than a dozen sentences to me.

Not only did she become mute, but she changed physically. One day she seemed disfigured. She was no longer elegant; she was hunched over, her hair pulled tightly into a bun; she had rings under her eyes; and she was pale and thin.

Then the changes became even more drastic. She no longer looked after herself at all; her clothes were grimy and stained; she seemed smaller; her shoulders were stiff and high, as if she were trying to bury her skull. Her gaze was vacant and very sad.

All I could do was watch her decline. I had told her to see a doctor and she had answered that she didn't want to see anyone, especially not a doctor. She had added that I could continue to come if I wanted, but that I could just as easily not. I was upset.

I would ring the doorbell and she would let me in. I would bring her flowers, fruit, sweets. She would thank me. She would arrange the flowers in a vase, but would never touch anything else. The following day my little gifts would have disappeared. The flowers would fade, the water would stagnate. I would sit in the armchair. She would sit in her usual spot, on a cushion, her back against the wall, her head tilted forward, staring at her hands. Beside her lay an ashtray, cigarettes and a lighter. Sometimes she would ask me to bring her cigarettes. When I suggested that she was smoking too much, she just smiled at me and shrugged as if to say that it didn't matter, that my concern was absurd, that everything was absurd.

The situation got worse and worse. I became seriously worried about her. She disconnected the telephone. Laure wasn't in Paris, and I didn't know how to get hold of her. I tried to get Elsa to tell me Laure's address, and this time she found her voice: 'Leave her alone. Laure has nothing to do with this. No one is making you come here. I don't need anyone taking care of me.'

One day she didn't answer the door when I rang. I was afraid; I thought something might have happened to her. And then I realised the key was in the door. I went in. There wasn't a sound. She wasn't in the sitting room or the kitchen.

Her bedroom door was shut. I had never been in there. She was in bed; she didn't turn her head toward me, but her eyes were open and she was breathing. On the beside table there was an empty coffee cup and an ashtray full of cigarette ends.

Our silence and inertia pervaded the room. We were imprisoned by the suffocating oppressiveness of the absence of word or action. That's all there was. Her suicide was present, almost visible, lying next to her. My powerlessness was also present, standing at my side. I was terrified. I had no right to help her in spite of herself. She knew what she was doing.

I went into the kitchen. There was nothing to eat, only a large packet of coffee and some sugar. Piled up on the table were all the little things I had brought on my visits: biscuits, records, pictures, books, pots of jam, chocolate bars. She hadn't touched a thing. That miscellany was our only conversation, our only interaction: I deposited my gifts in the sitting room and she brought them in here, but the packages were intact. No, there was something else: all the flowers accumulated in the sitting room, faded, dried, rotting – she hadn't thrown any of them out. And then, most important of all, there was the key in the door. I existed for her. Never had my existence meant so much to anyone, I was sure of it. What did she expect of me?

The next day I brought the tape recorder with me. I no longer knew what to bring her. Nothing interested her; she didn't even look at me. That morning I saw the machine at home in the hall and picked it up. I put it on the beside table beside the cigarettes. She didn't move but she knew that I was there. I think she knew.

The scene was the same for three days in a row, exactly the same: the key in the door, her in her bedroom, shrivelled up on her bed. I don't think she was even drinking coffee any more. She smoked. I emptied her ashtray and every day there were new cigarette ends. She was in danger. I was certain that she was going under, that she was about to die.

One morning I noticed that the tape recorder had been moved. I saw that the cassette had been used. I rewound it, and pressed the play button. Her voice came on. At first it was lifeless, but then she had forced herself, extended herself. Her voice replaced all the silence, filling up the space, yelling:

'I am nothing . . . I am nothing . . . I am nil . . . I am zero . . . I am zero, a round empty space, a hollow . . . I'm not a zero that is useful as a starting point for plus and minus, the origin of infinity . . . I'm a zero that cancels out . . . I am a void, my void . . . I am useless, absolutely useless . . .'

She heard her voice, and her body on the bed became what she said: nothing, a worthless heap, a rag, a shed skin.

My intuition told me that if I did not do something crucial in the next few seconds, this woman would die. Depending on what I did, she would be born here on her bed, or she would die. That life or death depended on me. I remembered the wave in which she had rolled as a child, in which she had lost her footing, in which she had lost her sense of up and down, of right side up and upside down, of beginning and end, in which she had suffocated, until she felt a bit of the solid beach, just barely, and then the urgency of regaining her footing came over her – otherwise it would have been the end. I had to be that little bit of solid beach, that feeling of *terra firma*. I had to do something; I couldn't let the wave carry her off forever. In the intensity of my feeling, I was afraid of acting; I didn't know how to act. I had to hurry, that was all. Her voice stopped yelling.

I heard myself saying, 'At least you were able to rescue your daughter.'

And as I said it, I thought that I had lost everything.

Now there was only the soft hiss of the blank tape as it continued to turn. But the silence no longer had the same quality about it. It wasn't compact; on the contrary, it was fluid.

She said, 'Whoever said I rescued my daughter?'

'I don't know how Laure was rescued, you never told me. I suppose that she was rescued and that you were the one who did it.'

'I wasn't the one who rescued Laure. She rescued herself.'

'Well, it just goes to show that I can't finish the book on my own.'

She smiled. Life had returned with those words, and that made both of us happy. We took advantage of it as one takes advantage of the sun in winter, of something precious that must be protected. She held out her hand and I grasped it in mine. I sat on the edge of the bed and took her in my arms. She let me. I rocked her. She was thin. I was afraid of letting go, afraid that it would start all over again. She murmured: 'I'm going to talk, I'm going to talk . . . For three years I watched everything I held dear crumble, everything that had given my life a framework. I'm not the type who knows how to live from day to day without a care. I need to believe . . . That's why I wanted to tell the story, to try to regain the desire to believe. I feel I can believe in you . . . I'm going to talk . . .'

Her eyes were shut and she kept repeating, 'I'm going to talk, I'm going to talk.'

Elsa was a strong woman: ten days later she was back on her feet again.

I continued to visit her daily, but she soon asked me not to come any more. She wanted to be alone. My zeal touched her and intrigued her, but also embarrassed her. She said as much. She said that sooner or later she would have to talk about her embarrassment but that she didn't want to for the time being. She rang me every evening; she told me she was working, writing some things and taping some.

During that period, I thought about her, loving thoughts. I was jealous. But of what? Of whom? Of Laure? Would I have liked to be Elsa's child? Of her fighting spirit? How could I envy the fog in which she was living? Of her solitude? Of her lucidity? I envied her obstinacy, her commitment, her will to seek, the passion that she put into everything, that consumed her, that was her undoing. I missed her.

Two weeks later, she asked me to come over. I found her changed: splendid, cheerful, in good shape.

On the low table in the sitting room she had built a structure out of sheets of paper and cassettes, a sort of multi-tiered pagoda. Cassettes, paper, cassettes, paper – each layer was numbered.

Laughing, she said, 'I've made you a Big Mac: a layer of lettuce, a layer of cheese, a layer of tomato, a layer of bacon, topped with ketchup. A regular rubbish heap! I've arranged it all in the order I produced it, chronologically, but there is no real order. I don't know if you'll be able to make anything of it.'

It was as if what had happened during her time of distress had been swept away, erased, as if she had never been in distress. It wasn't a taboo subject; she didn't hide it. It was simply the past. I no longer knew if I should admire her strength or lament that she had regained it. I remembered the day I rocked her, when I had the impression that she was tiny and I was restoring her to life . . . In handing her jumble of words over to me, she seemed to deprive me of that memory. She had re-established the exact distance that there had been between us before.

I set to work immediately. In two days I had cleaned up the first few cassettes. They were full on both sides, full of hesitations and silences. She had stopped the machine frequently. Her sentences were broken by sharp clicks of the tape stopping and starting. At the beginning of the first cassette there was still the 'I am nothing, I am zero . . .' She hadn't erased it. At my place, her voice existed all the time. Distorted by the machine, it wasn't as beautiful as in reality, but I compensated mentally and managed to hear it as it was. I imagined that she was there, speaking to me.

I extracted a few pages, which I delivered to her. She took them; settled in amongst her cushions, as usual, and read them aloud.

'I don't want to go into detail about what happened during the three years of hell when Laure was a drug addict. It was too miserable, too painful. And yet those details dwell in me; they are what stop me. I don't know what lesson I'm supposed to learn from them. I'm unable to explain how a drug addict kicks the habit. I'm incapable, scientifically, of helping someone to stop taking drugs. Despite all I've been through and learnt, I'm not capable of giving advice and even less capable of devising a method . . .

'Other people frighten me now . . . People behave badly with drug addicts. They become aggressive . . . People are nasty to drug addicts. I think they see themselves when they look at them. They see their own worst side and can't accept

101

it . . . In users, all human capacity for spinelessness is nurtured by drugs.

'It wasn't long before Laure's friends invaded the flat. They came to kick the habit, but they never managed to do it. Each time we left Paris, we took some of them with us. I lived with no one but drug addicts for three years.

'Drug addicts are liars, thieves, hypocrites. They're careless, sly . . . They sell themselves. They destroy themselves, and at the same time, destroy everything around them. People say, "They have no will-power. It's a question of will-power . . . If they wanted to they could stop . . . Things are too easy for them, they're like spoilt children . . . They need to suffer a little . . . A good war would straighten them out . . ." These people are wrong. Drug addicts are seriously ill and they're mutants . . . mainly mutants . . . But they themselves don't even know they're mutating. They spout old, vaguely leftish political ideas or, alternatively, frankly reactionary ones. They're a new generation, but all they talk about is their parents, never themselves and who they are. If they did, they would soon stop taking drugs and it's our minds that would be blown. They're manipulated, but not the way they say they are . . .

'And then there's money . . . They have a strange relationship with money, a fanatical relationship. The golden calf exists. They live that, that frantic, alienating adoration . . . Everything is money, because anything can be traded for drugs . . . Living with drug addicts is living with money, bank notes, cheques, coins, the prices of things, the liquidity of money, its precariousness, its abundance, its absence. Everything depends on the imminence of the next hit . . . It's like the tide . . . It's exhausting . . . Money is sacred . . . to everyone . . . It's vital . . . I began to defend my money like a madwoman . . . I was robbed of everything . . . I began to lie, to hide my every penny like a miser . . . I didn't know how duplicitous I could be, nor how greedy. I didn't think I was like that at all . . . I looked at the value of things differently.

'There's also the hidden face of desire that, to them, is desire itself. An amorous relationship with the needle, the syringe . . . Heroin addicts, real junkies, have no sex life, or rather their sexuality is no longer expressed through their sex organs; heroin destroys that life and makes another type of sexuality develop . . . A perversity . . . There is only one sex organ, the same for boys and girls, the penetrating type. It's very thin, very pointed, very small, shiny, metallic. It ejaculates powder diluted in water warmed over the flame of a candle . . . They play with their blood endlessly . . . They draw in a little, it mixes with the heroin in the syringe, colouring it – almost caressing it – then they pump it out and draw it in again . . . They're fascinated by the in and out, for as long as they can resist their desire . . . They have no other desire. They think of nothing but heroin, talk of nothing but heroin: the quality, where it comes from, the quantity, the price, the effects . . . Overdoses are described down to the smallest detail . . . Instead of bringing them down, it excites them. When someone they know dies, they increase their dose. But if one of them tries to kick the habit, or manages to kick the habit, everything possible is done to get the person back or to deny the person's escape . . . Heroin is fatal. It is their fate. They imagine no other, they want no other . . . And yet they talk about quitting . . . When it has satisfied them, they think they've had enough because they've just enjoyed it. So they talk about rejecting it because it's too expensive, because it torments them. That's when they're lucid, and know it for what it is: vile filth. At first, when I realised that, when I saw that Laure was aware of it, I thought I could build on that awareness . . . But as soon as the effect of the drug wears off and they no longer feel its warmth, when instead, the cold of withdrawal sets in, or even just the idea of that cold, they begin to desire nothing but heroin . . . They can't do without it . . . They would rather die of one last fix than not have any.

'And then there's their bodies . . . It's incredible how they're both close to and remote from their bodies. The liberties they take with them . . . The trust they have in the pharmacopoeia; every drug addict is a walking pharmacy . . . Some of them vomit a lot. They say it cleans them out, purifies them. They don't say that heroin has destroyed their livers. They don't say it because they don't believe it. Only old people have liver trouble. Addicts' bodies are their veins, nothing but tangles of red and blue. Their only physical problem is the fragility of the pathways of their venous systems. The ones who are worried about the police inject themselves in their gums . . . They inject themselves anywhere. Sometimes they make a game of shooting into an unlikely vein. Heroin suppresses the appetite, so users eat rarely and poorly. Their bones become decalcified, their teeth rot. They shoot up with old syringes, ones that have just been used, ones they find lying around, any one at all will do. They become infected, they have abscesses, they suffer. Heroin eases their pain. Their skin dries out and ages very quickly. They see themselves, they see themselves ageing, and they have to go to the country: "Oh, the country, fantastic!" As soon as they can, they get some provisions together and take off. There's always an empty country house somewhere in France belonging to an innocent family or a knowing friend. They pretend to play in the grass like the children they still are, but they are exhausted children, dying children, and they soon come back to nurse at their pointed bottle, locking themselves up behind closed shutters, because the light of day is too painful for them.'

She stopped and looked for a hankie in her skirt pocket.

Very soon after she had begun to read, she had started to cry. At first I didn't notice. I thought that something was bothering her, that she was trying to remove a speck or an eyelash from her eye somehow, first with one hand and then with the other. Then I saw that her cheeks were glistening and there was a tear sliding across her temple into her hair. She was crying too much. She let her tears flow; she stopped wiping them away.

'My tears are soft . . . They do me good. I feel as though I'm taking a bath . . . a nice warm bath . . .'

She bathed in her water without moving, without speaking. She went off, far away, for a long time. Then she came back and began to read again: 'They dress and make themselves up with a freedom I envy, boys as well as girls. Drug addicts are monstrances for heroin. Nothing is too good for heroin, too precious, too dazzling, too colourful, too wild . . . When they're drugged they're like mad people . . . magnificent mad people . . . distressing exhibitionists . . . When they perfume themselves they're perfuming the drug . . . It's touching to see them go off, laughing, with their ribbons, spangles and scents. Each of them is a celebration, a carnival, a parade . . . They return with a chill in their bones, mascara streaked across their made-up faces . . . their clothes in disarray . . . ladders in their stockings . . . heels broken . . . They run.

'Raids are a common feature of their lives: police round-ups, dealers tracking them, debts hounding them, petty break-ins, withdrawal at their heels . . . They run, jump, dash across streets, dodging cars . . . They can do the most amazing stunts . . . Their bodies are exhausted by drugs, eaten away from all sides . . . Their kidneys, their livers, their lungs, their hearts, their endocrine systems – everything's ravaged by drugs. And yet with those bodies they can set records. Their bodies harbour an unbelievable desire, an . . . unacceptable . . . incomprehensible energy . . . That is the energy that destroyed me. I tried to understand it. I couldn't. I failed . . .'

She came to the end of the pages I had brought. She straightened up and turned to me, smiling.

'I failed, I haven't got over it yet . . . What's next?'

'The description of Professor Greffier.'

'Oh yes, that's right. What did you do with it?'

'I left it almost exactly as you wrote it, except for the odd comma.'

'I couldn't say that aloud, I couldn't bear to hear myself saying it. It's too private. It had to be written; it required the silence of writing, the secrecy of writing. It's not too academic?'

'Not at all. Quite the opposite. You've made an effort. It's good, you'll see. It's in the same style as what I've been writing.'

We both laughed. It was good to laugh. She laughed like a child. Then she said, almost excusing herself: 'I'd like to keep moving ahead on my own for a while. I'm trying to see myself as a whole. I scare myself. I'd rather read this when I'm rested and alone.'

We agreed to meet again a week later in the afternoon. I left her with her pages.

Professor Greffier

He was sitting there on the sofa.

Well, it wasn't exactly a sofa, it was more of a love-seat, neither an armchair nor a couch: a low upholstered seat without arms.

His seat, along with another similar one and a third longer one that sat four – all in dark leather – was part of a set arranged around an ugly square table made of fake copper, some cheap metal that was losing its shine in spots, covered with a thin sheet of glass; a piece of junk that had been left in his flat.

He was sitting there on his dark leather sofa . . .

His cats had scratched the leather so much in some spots that they'd gone right through it. Woolly stuffing was popping out through the holes they had made. But it was nice, thick, soft leather.

He was sitting there on his sofa. I could see the scratches; I could see the marks of the creatures' frenzy on the corner of the backrest, right near his head.

I was sitting next to him, on the end of the long sofa, right next to him. I had been about to speak when the ravaged back had caught my eye, and now I couldn't say a thing. I couldn't find the words; I searched, but nothing that came to mind was exactly what I wanted to say. 'I'm leaving, I'm leaving you, I never want to see you again, I shall never see you again, it's all over . . .' None of it fitted. It was what I had come to say, but it was no longer exactly what I felt. Now that I was there, I wanted to say something else as well, but I didn't know what. I didn't want to talk about Laure, or the state she was in. He wasn't interested in Laure; he wasn't interested in anyone, except me, because he sensed that I was getting away from him. I couldn't use Laure as a pretext. My desire to leave him was old, older than the problem with Laure. I had always been careful to keep my two lives separate, and there was no reason to start mixing them now that it was all over.

I was fascinated by the gashes, by the strands of fraying whitish material poking out through them. The wounds were a trap. Because of them I was caught, bound by the memory of days that had turned into weeks, months, years, almost two decades. As if the furniture's scars symbolised the time we had spent together, and as if I couldn't face never seeing them again. I couldn't understand what had come over me. Why the feeling of danger? Why the fear?

As I was talking and dredging up the memories that provided the raw material for the one hundred and forty-three pages – believing that I could thereby rid myself of this feeling of helplessness – the memory of that fear often returned. I chased it away. I didn't have the courage to face it. Now I think that I won't make any progress unless I do face it.

I was going to leave, I was going to leave him. But because I believed for so long that he was my haven, a certain sadness began to fill the penumbra of the sombre flat. A man, a haven; a man, a lecher . . .

An incomprehensible nostalgia for this stinking haven, for its *rouilles*,* came over me. Nostalgia for the shelter where the deep water is calm. Yet if the problem with Laure hadn't arisen, I might well have stayed forever. Now I had to tell him I was weighing anchor. I would not sneak off. It was over! I was leaving, I was heading for the open sea!

But I didn't say a word.

He was sitting there on the sofa. His body had shaped the seat until no one else could sit on it, since he didn't really so much sit on it as sprawl. He had formed depressions by flopping his hundred kilos and one metre ninety into it, then coiling up, folding his long thin legs against his high pot belly. He would nestle his long, heavy head in a hollow in

* A pungent Mediterranean sauce served with fish soups and stews.

the back that his hair had oiled and blackened over time, just above the spot the cats had clawed to shreds.

He always had cats, she-cats.

For the last few years they had been living in the nooks and crannies of the flat. He didn't try to find them any more; they no longer interested him, but that hadn't always been the case. I wondered if the desire to leave him had not come to me at the same time as he lost his interest in the cats; or had he perhaps lost interest in them because he sensed that I wanted to leave? He had a very sure instinct for vital rhythms. He always had female cats, never male, although he sometimes talked affectionately about a tom he had once had, named Berlingot.

When I first knew him, he had two Siamese cats, degenerate beasts. One hadn't a single tooth in her head; she had been born like that, and she ate only what her sister spat up. The two of them spent their time dealing with their feeding problem. One chewed for a long time whatever she found in her dish, then forced herself to regurgitate half of it. The other lapped up this pulp. They were revolting, yet touching because of their solidarity. They wouldn't have been able to survive without each other. In exchange for the regurgitated food, the one with no teeth licked her sister, kept her clean, suckled her, and took care of her as if she had been her kitten. They had wound up with him the same way the square table in the sitting room had, abandoned. Refuse.

At the time when I was going to his place every day, when it had become my office in a way (since it was the secretarial work I did for him that enabled me to continue my studies), I often wondered why so many people insisted on leaving things there: the cats, the sitting room table, a moped, a complete suite of dining room furniture, and all sorts of other furniture and objects, things that were useless to him, and generally ugly. Why did they? Because he had so many big empty rooms? Were they simply rubbish or were they more like traces? When I later asked him why, he answered, 'Why not? I don't give a damn.'

The flat, carefully dusted by the concierge, who came in and out without being noticed, looked like a showroom. All the curios increased the feeling of emptiness that the place gave me. On some tense days, it seemed as if ghosts and sighs were rising from this hotchpotch, of accounts being settled, perhaps, of abortions, of something oppressive, a whole life dead and buried: a cemetery.

Women had left all these things. Women from his family, old mistresses, new mistresses, women who no longer mattered to him. Sometimes they came to the flat. Usually I didn't meet them. They didn't stay long. He would dress up to receive them, and behave with unusual urbanity. I could hear him. He would invite them into the sitting room, then lead them to the room where whatever they had left was kept. They would whisper – it sounded as if they were in church – and they would go, leaving a strong fragrance behind them, as if they had been spraying perfume. Why? To linger? To remain there still, despite themselves, despite him? They would leave; some of them would never come back, but their objects would remain, behind closed shutters, as motionless as sentries.

He had no children.

Sometimes he would 'stroke' his cats. The urge to touch them would suddenly come over him, an intense need he couldn't resist. I was never able to determine what stirred this desire in him; perhaps nothing did. Perhaps it was like a heartbeat or a blink of an eye – an involuntary, vital action.

All of a sudden he would get up from his desk and try to catch one or even both if he could. It wasn't easy because they would run away from him; they were afraid of him.

First he would shut the doors and then run around after them. He would hunt them down. They would scramble away in fright. In the space of a few seconds, the room would become a jungle, a savannah for a safari, a firing range. It was brutal and perverse – a guerilla war. He was huge, enormous; they were scrawny but lively. He would wrap his hands in newspaper, because they scratched, bit, spat. Despite these precautions, he always had a few bites or scratches on his hands, pink marks that he sometimes stroked. At times like this, I didn't exist; I could be only an obstacle, if anything.

I usually remained at my typewriter. Sometimes he would

get up when we were in the middle of a sentence. He would leave me hanging, and it was as though I had disappeared from the room. He would devote himself unreservedly to his hunt, without any preliminaries. He would indulge himself completely in the indecency of his irresistible impulse. It was indecent because I was watching, indecent to me only because I stayed; I could have left. He was caught in the throes of an overwhelming desire; he couldn't help himself; he had to satisfy it no matter what. He didn't resist it; he abandoned himself to it. Jubilation mixed with suffering came over his features and was evident in his gestures. His enormous, puffy, fissured face became animated. The chaos of his usually sagging features became firmer. His existence, like a candle, had left traces in the form of fleshy drips, telltale signs of the laughter of bygone days, bawdy clarity, but also fragility, wounded tenderness, and even the nightmares and breathtaking discoveries of childhood. Despite his ugliness, his face was moving, deeply moving. During the chase, a certain beauty appeared in his face – freshness, exhilaration, vulnerability . . . I felt I was surprising him as he had been before the ravages of time had done their work – intact. And unforgettable. No matter what happens now, I shall never forget what I saw there: his moments of utter madness, his insane savagery, his frenzied hope, his petulant cruelty, his joy in taking and torturing. Unforgettable. Always, as an excuse, at the worst moments of hatred, the echo of this innocence returned to me, calming my anger, prompting my forgiveness, making me agree to stay.

Until I could no longer agree to it. Or rather, until he lost the power to make me stay.

He was sitting there on his sofa, a fallen man, pitiful. I'm leaving. That's what I have come to tell him; I am leaving for good, forever. Nothing ties me to him any longer. I see his haggard face and the old age that has worked on it, undermining it, washing it away. It has been worn out from within; the sags in his flesh are empty – skin hangs against skin; the muscles have disappeared with their blood; the paleness and pinkness of the aged has spread throughout his body.

I never saw him give up a struggle. It might take him a while, but he always managed to capture them eventually. His paper gloves would be in shreds, and he would shake them off quickly with cat-like movements. His hands and wrists would be bleeding. And then the torture would begin. He would force the cats into degrading positions – usually with their heads shoved between their hind legs. At that point the animals would let him do what he wanted; they would lay their ears flat and snarl with hatred, nothing more. They wouldn't strike at him with their paws; their claws would be out, but relaxed. Once they were in that position – their muzzles jammed into their arseholes, more or less – he would caress them with long repetitive strokes, while clamping their jaws shut. One after the other the fingers of his free hand would stretch out, bend supplely. He would move them back and forth along the stiff upright fur of the Siamese cats, stroking them spasmodically. Then he would let them go and wouldn't bother with them any more. He wouldn't even watch them run away.

It was an ugly spectacle, extremely ugly, and yet I felt there was a certain logical necessity to it. I was annoyed with myself for that, but that's how it was. During the whole time of the hunt, I was repulsed by him, and I would say to myself: 'It's all over, I can't work with him any longer. He's disgusting, revolting.' And then at the end, despite the cats' torture – or perhaps because of it – I suddenly felt relieved, satisfied in a way. Everything was all right, and we would begin to work again without making the slightest reference to what had just happened.

Then I finally told him I would no longer work with him.

*

Elsa didn't know that I was in the process of becoming her shadow, her double, her echo. She didn't know that her voice was living with me. She had no idea how intimate I was with her. I played certain parts of the tapes over and over, not to listen to them, but to hear them. For example: 'The first day, acting like a Guide captain . .' I knew it all by heart. I no longer paid any attention to the words: I heard the inflections of her voice, the depth of her voice. I heard what was left unsaid.

I was really getting to know her. I was sure I wasn't inventing her.

Elsa was both extremely curious and extremely methodical. She could make progress only by organising what she knew: what she had learnt and what she had guessed, mostly what she had guessed. She knew things first by her gut feelings, but she was wary of them. Elsa was a faint-hearted adventurer; her appetite for adventure was as great as her timidity. The woman who spoke alone into the microphone needed everything she had got to find her direction. She needed to understand in order to act, but not to think. Her thought was free, but her reasoning wasn't. Each time she let her imagination or sense of adventure run wild, she would justify the liberty she had taken in the next sentence. I tried to imagine what hell she had gone through with Laure. I tried to imagine her frenzied desire to love no matter what, to love Laure on drugs, with drugs, because of drugs, her frenzied desire to understand drugs. She had to understand drugs if she was to continue to love her daughter. She would not have given up on Laure for all the money in the world, but nothing in the world could have made her accept junk. She had lived three years crushed by that constraint. She had held out through love, solely through love; a mad, pure love . . .

I wanted to love her and I wanted her to love me . . .

The day I took her the transcripts of tapes 4 and 5, I was like a madman. I had just spent eight days of madness with her. Eight days and nights. Eight days reassuring her, protecting her, helping her become happy, dreaming of her happy. But it was my kind of happiness. Would she want anything to do with it? In any case, things couldn't go on like this any longer. I had made up my mind to put it to her.

She was normal, she was reasonable, although slightly worried, too.

'Is there anything about Professor Greffier in what you've brought me?'

112

'Yes, one passage.'

'You didn't rearrange it too much? In the part you gave me last time, it seemed to me you'd cut a little . . . And I don't think I was that crude . . . I don't have a copy . . .'

'I didn't really change anything, no. Would you like me to bring you the original?'

'No, don't bother. I believe you. It can be disturbing to give birth to oneself . . . frightening . . . I should know, though . . . What are we going to do with all this? Are we going to use it?'

'I think it's essential.'

'In what form? It can't stay as it is, it's indecent. The pages you left me last time were simply indecent.'

'That's not the word I would use. Immodest, perhaps. You often are . . .'

'You'll put it into context, as they say, won't you?'

'Yes, probably. I don't know. It's hard to say since we still haven't got to the end yet. For the time being I can't do the same thing I did for the hundred and forty-three pages. There are things missing. I don't know how it ends.'

'How shall we go about finishing up?'

'However you wish. Using the tape recorder or some other method. You can write; or I can come over, you can talk and I can take notes, as we did before.'

'What do you think?'

'I'd rather come here. I've had a listen to the rest of the tapes, but I couldn't follow it all. It's confusing. There's some repetition. I'd like to go over it in detail.'

'The idea of a book scares me.'

'Why?'

'Because it's public. I don't like to make a spectacle of myself.'

'Don't worry. Reading is a very private activity. People read only what they want to read. It's almost as if they read only what is already written inside them. We live with our fantasies.'

'Obviously . . . So you're going to make a *coquecigrue* of me.'

'What's that?'

'It's an old word that used to mean a legendary bird, a fantasy . . .'

'You must have read that in Freud.'

'I don't remember. Probably in Jung . . . Anyway, we're not there yet. I shudder at the thought of what you've made of my ramblings.'

As she had the last time, she took the pages and read aloud.

'Often, to kick heroin, addicts drink.

'But heroin is so strong that they need enormous amounts of alcohol to reach a state similar to the one they would be in with a single shot of heroin.

'Once, one of the first times we went off together – it was just after I left Professor Greffier – Laure waited in the car below while I was with him . . . we ended up in a house in Normandy that friends had lent me.

'On the way back from Morocco I'd realised that I couldn't stay in Paris and that I wouldn't have enough money for us to go off on trips like the one to Morocco, so I called some people I knew who had country houses. It was the off-season, and the houses were empty . . . I ended up with a list of refuges all over France.

'This one, in Normandy, was still being built. It was empty . . . Fortunately it had a fireplace. Apart from that, there were two beds, a table, a few chairs. Outside it was foggy.

'I intended to stay there for as long as Laure's therapy required . . . I didn't get that far. I had been too shaken up, too overwhelmed. I had had to face too many things at once. When I promised to help her that first day, I had committed myself to therapy with her . . . I would get her to talk, I would listen to her, I would help her become aware of the source of her illness . . . At the time I believed that addiction was a neurosis like any other . . . that it was a disorder for which there was a therapeutic solution . . . that together we would discover where her energy had skidded off the rails, where it had escaped . . . You know I'm interested in entropy . . . You know that I've developed a method . . . and that I obtain, or rather I have obtained, interesting results with young children . . . Anyway, I wanted to proceed that way with Laure . . .

'When we arrived in Normandy, Laure reacted badly to the tranquillisers she was taking to help her give up. She was agitated and anxious. I was starting to find out how duplicitous drug addicts can be. I suspected that she wasn't taking her pills, or that she wasn't taking her full doses, so that she would have an excuse to go back to Paris, where she could get some heroin. I asked questions to see whether my suspicions had any basis. She flew into a rage. She cried. She screamed that I was treating her like a child, that she was there to kick the habit and that under these conditions, if I didn't trust her, she would never be able to do it . . . There was something wrong. We talked. I explained to her that my plan was to stay there until she was really better, several months perhaps, that work on the house would not begin again until the spring. She agreed. That's when alcohol came into the picture . . .

'I didn't make the connection with the morphine that she had demanded in Marseilles . . .

'We went to the nearest village and bought some gin. I bought the largest bottle, thinking that Laure would have enough for a month. It was ten o'clock in the morning. By three in the afternoon the bottle was empty. Laure began to calm down . . . We went to buy another at around five o'clock because she started to feel ill again. She had taken a few pills, and I was afraid of the mix. The stores close early in the country . . .

'Just as during her first night of withdrawal in Hyères, I was shocked. My mind could not accept what I saw. The amount of alcohol and tranquillisers she had absorbed should have wiped her out, and yet she wasn't wiped out at all – I was . . . I felt that we should leave the house, that things were beginning to go wrong, that she was slowly killing herself . . . But in Laure's mind, on the other hand, there was no question of leaving. She had brought some records and a record-player that she turned up to full volume. I remember a woman's voice shouting "Horses! Horses!" . . . On the album cover was a picture of the singer: a woman with a thin, distressing, beautiful face and a free body; a gangly figure with huge arms and legs that seemed to have acquired their own independence, that were apparently free from the shackles of the shoulder and hip joints . . . Laure danced alone in front of the fire. She was ravishing, she was happy.

'And she talked. She talked about the woman who was singing, who had since died of an overdose, about other music and other voices, all dead. All drug addicts. They had all gone to the end of the heroin road: saints, heroes, legends.

'I listened very attentively. She was praising the void. I was the one who thought she was praising the void, she didn't use that term: she was talking about a way of life and she venerated all the symbols of that life . . . that void.

'The torrent of words rushing out of her created a frightening distance between us. Not the right distance, not the distance required for therapy; no, an aggressive distance . . . First she was a stranger and then as the days passed, as the gin bottles emptied, she became an enemy. I was against what she was saying, I was the enemy of that life she was singing about, dancing for, talking about. But I kept all that to myself. I noted it, nothing more. I hoped I would be able to calm down, find my objectivity again, listen neutrally . . .

'She never seemed drunk. She was brimming with alcohol but she didn't stagger, she had no difficulty speaking, she was perfectly lucid . . . I was never so close to abandoning her, to breaking our contract. I hated those people who were singing. I hated the beauty of Laure's body possessed by their rhythms. I hated their lyrics. I hated myself staring into the fire, incapable of getting a grip on myself, falling asleep out of fatigue, there on the floor, in front of the fireplace, waking up frozen to the marrow because the fire had gone out. Laure was asleep in a bed, probably dead drunk, full of tranquillisers . . .

'The first day, acting like a Guide captain, I had drawn up a plan of activities to help Laure regain the healthy use of her body. I'd said to her: "You used to be an athlete. You should start exercising again. You used to enjoy physical exercise. It would do you good to channel your energy into simple worthwhile work." She had agreed with the idea. "As long as you don't suggest any competitions, all right, because I couldn't care less any more whether I'm first or last." The fire was actually a good excuse for this type of exercise. Going to fetch wood in the nearby forest, bringing it back to the house, sawing it, splitting it – we didn't do it all just for form's sake; the fireplace was our only source of heat. She agreed, and at first she came with me, but she was so thin and weak that she soon felt ill, so I wound up going alone.

'Fetching firewood was the only activity that offered me refuge. It rained constantly. I would go out, eagerly filling my lungs with the damp, humus-scented air, and my thoughts would be racing as I looked for dead branches, trees smothered by others, covered with lichen, that had fallen down, their roots exposed. I kept thinking of Laure, how to go about having some sort of reasonable conversation with her, the need to become calm and patient again. I would return to the house full of plans, with a new strategy. As soon as I reached the field around the house, I would hear music. I would find Laure asleep, or dancing, or reading a comic . . . She obviously wanted nothing to do with my therapy. Then what on earth were we doing out there in the deserted countryside? The distance between us was greater than ever.

'There was nothing really wrong with what she was doing. I had no reason to lay down the law, to impose my order. She knew all about my order. I had no answer for her when she asked, "Why do we have to wash up right after eating? Why can't we do it later?" All I could say was, "Because that's how it is," so it was better not to say anything.

'If our conversation turned to the fact that I had a profession, that I earned my own living, she would launch into pseudo-political speeches that implied it was time for a revolution.

' "Laure, would you go off to Paris now and work for a revolution?"

' "With whom?"

' "With extremists, with groups that want revolution."

' "They're all a bunch of crack-pots! The Marxist-Leninists are all screwed up! The Maoists are all screwed up! Communists are even more reactionary than official reactionaries . . ."

'I had no influence over her. When we talked about life, about happiness, we were talking about two different ways of life, two different types of happiness. We had absolutely nothing in common on a philosophical level. And I couldn't keep my mouth shut. I would start out listening, and then, after a while, I couldn't help myself – I would butt in and then hear myself spewing out these dismayingly moralistic speeches . . .

'Her moods were very unstable. She would fly into terrible rages, positively abnormal. She would scream: "It's just like the washing up! What makes you think your ideas are any better than mine?" . . . I knew that I shouldn't barricade myself behind my principles, my knowledge, my certainties, that I should try to enter into her world. She trusted me. She spoke openly of her experience as a drug addict. She wanted to leave that life behind because of all the material constraints involved, because of withdrawal, because of money, but at the same time she was attracted by what heroin represented, by the void. To reach her, I had to understand what that void was. I saw only the void, nothingness, death. What was so seductive in that? I had to take a step towards her instead of always trying to get her to come towards me.

'One day when I went shopping, I bought some champagne. I said to myself that I would drink a little. I don't drink much. And in my mind champagne was associated with parties, with dissolute living. I thought that if I led a dissolute life for a while, I might find a way of reaching Laure. So I bought a case of champagne. The local wine merchant was offering a "fantastic special" to launch a new brand: "Fourteen bottles for the price of twelve!"

'What a party we had! The first cork flew, and we clinked glasses in front of the fireplace. The champagne soon started to take effect and I became very merry. We danced, we fell into each other's arms. Yes, yes, we found each other again. It was heaven. I listened and finally managed to reply calmly to her questions, while she filled my glass . . . But I can't hold drink. To be able to keep going all night, I went and made myself sick and then drank some more. I was drunk, but she wasn't. She laughed, she made fun of me, saying, "You don't know how to drink!" She explained very reasonably the morality of using drugs, the economics of getting high, the best means of reaching the void.

' "And then what?"

' "And then nothing. It's a void – what more do you want? You're stoned, and nothing matters any more."

' "And when you come down?"

' "You start over."

' "Until it kills you."

' "Of course! You have to die anyway, so you might just as well die like that as working eight hours a day for sixty-five years!"

'That kind of reasoning made us laugh until we cried.

'The next day I had a frightful hangover and felt like killing myself. Laure had only the memory of a great evening. She was protective.

' "Elsa, the best way to get over a binge is to have another drink when you wake up."

' "But don't you understand that my body, and especially my mind, functioned last night because of the specific properties of alcohol and that I need alcohol today to keep on functioning the same way? Don't you understand that if I have a drink now, it's the alcohol that will make me function and not myself? Don't you understand that it's the same with heroin, that it's not you who exist, but the drug that's in your place?"

' "And don't *you* understand that it's the same with money, a career, success, the family, beauty, religion! It's never you who exist; it's what gives you your energy that exists; it's the carrot that you're running after. What makes the daily grind any better than drugs? What makes God any better than drugs? What makes work, family and country any better than drugs? What? At least druggies are druggies, people living their own lives. Druggies aren't nice respectable bourgeois; they aren't hypocrites! And that bothers the hell out of everybody."

'The wall, the brick wall. The dog chasing its own tail.

Words drowning each other out; certainties becoming diluted. May 1968 without the hope . . .

' "You see, Laure, what shocks me is what drugs do to your body, the way they destroy your body. It's getting your body into such a state that there's no other solution but to have it treated by an organisation that you hate, to hand it over to something you hate. Going to hospital or prison, being arrested by the police or taken to a detox centre is such a degrading admission of failure. How can anyone accept that kind of a future?"

' "You're right. There are cowards everywhere. But many of the people who accept that only accept it cynically. It gives them a breather before starting all over again, or it protects them awhile from dealers who've got too dangerous . . . Not everyone has a mum who'll take them to the country . . . I'm not making fun of you, but I don't want to get involved in one of those schemes. If I don't manage to quit drugs . . . the minute I feel I'm incapable of quitting, I'll overdose."

' "But you do want to quit?"

' "Yes."

' "Why?"

' "Because it's too expensive."

' "Not because of what it is?"

' "But just what is it? It's no worse than alcohol or cigarettes, or jogging every morning! You know how many people they find in the Bois de Boulogne, in shorts and running shoes, who've had a heart attack? A lot more than there are ODs. You know how many alcoholics there are in France? You know how many people are killed on the roads by drunken drivers? You know how many French hospital beds are filled by alcoholics? Thousands, tens of thousands! You know how many smokers die of lung cancer or suffer from incurable respiratory ailments? Why does everyone make such a fuss about drugs? If a gram of heroin cost the same as a litre of wine or a packet of cigarettes, no one would ever mention heroin. Not only would no one talk about it, but there would be a national dope board, and a tax on dope, and advertising to make people buy dope: 'Fourteen grams for the price of twelve!' It's the price that shocks people and gives it that mystique. Dying of poverty is fine, dying in luxury is a tragedy! How ridiculous! Look how you've been buying me booze since we got here, when you would never buy me a hit of junk. You think getting pissed is better than shooting up?"

' "No, that's not the point. You know that."

' "All I know is that it's important because of what it costs. Because whatever's expensive is important. What the kids who come to see you say is important only because their parents have to pay a lot for it."

' "Now you're going too far, Laure!"

' "I'm not saying that money is important to you. I'm not saying that you take an interest in those kids because of the money, but it's important to the parents. They never realised their children had anything to say until they had to start coughing up! To me, *buying* junk is a problem, not using it. Apart from that, it's like flowers and incense in a church – it improves the atmosphere, that's all . . ."

'We never got beyond these simplistic conversations, hackneyed arguments from an outmoded form of protest. She refused to debate ideas and stuck to superficial provocation. And in my own way I did the same . . .

'We would stubbornly remain at that level. And often, to finish off, she would burst into tears, calling me horrid.

'When we returned to Paris, I was only a shadow of my former self.

'We sold her flat and she came to live with me.

'I tried to get help. I'd have given anything for help. But people avoided me. People avoid drug addicts. Drug addicts are embarrassing. Laure was right when she talked about money. People are willing to help those who would kill each other for a cheap bottle of booze, but they won't have anything to do with, or are ashamed of, those who would kill each other for a shot worth a thousand francs. That's the way it is. I don't know how many times people said to me: "You're too weak. You shouldn't give her a penny." I never did give her a penny, not directly, but she had a thousand and one ways to get money out of me. She would steal, or have one of her friends steal, anything of any value in the flat. Or I would write cheques to a driving school, for example, when in fact, she never took any driving lessons . . . She handled me very well. She never asked for money, only for cheques to take some course or other, or to pay a doctor who was fantastic at helping addicts kick the habit . . . Lots of tricks like that. Drug addicts are very well organised. They have all sorts of schemes wherever they are. There's no getting away from it . . . And when I pointed out that she wasn't fooling me, that I knew she was taking me for a ride, she replied: "Would you rather I do break-ins, or sell myself, or deal?"

'Feeling unable to save her, I consulted specialists, dozens of them. I asked all kinds of experts for advice, but they let me down. In the end they didn't want to talk to me any more. They left messages that they weren't there or that they would call me back, and they never did. Drug addicts bring us face to face with failure, with incompetence. That's not pleasant when you think you're competent.

'In any case, Laure wouldn't hear a word about therapy or detoxification in a hospital or anywhere else. I admit that I didn't press her too hard, because I saw so many of her friends come out of a cure and go right back to drugs the same day . . .

'The only people I could talk to were the police on the narcotics squad. There aren't many of them, and they're different from the rest of the police, who treat drug addicts like dogs. I've seen them do atrocious things . . . I've seen one of them kick a boy lying on the ground in the throes of withdrawal . . . I've seen another behaving obscenely with a girl in the same state, unable to defend herself. I've seen them dragging boys and girls by the hair into a police van . . . The officers on the narcotics squad aren't like that . . . They've seen all kinds . . . They see such misery . . . They don't know what the cure is; they don't know what to do, but in a way they understand the distress of drug addicts . . . They deserve some credit for that because drug addicts in distress do not always induce much sympathy. They're quick with abuse and fond of destructive reasoning, or else they're totally beaten down, completely indifferent . . . They're violent and dangerous when they're in withdrawal. They'd kill their mother and father for a hit . . . Once I answered my door and found myself face to face with two young men I didn't know. I heard a click: one of them had released the blade of a flick-knife – something I'd only ever seen in films. They came in, shutting the door behind them. They wanted money: Laure supposedly owed them money. I never found out whether it was true . . . They went over the flat, looking around for things to steal. They were in withdrawal, sweating . . . They wanted five thousand francs. For form's sake I haggled, and then quickly wrote out a cheque . . . Whatever do parents do who haven't any money? . . . It's true that dealers know the financial situation of their customers' families . . . The one with the knife said, "You got any cash?" I said no. "You've got cash – Let's see your handbag!" I gave them the bag. They took all my change from it. As they left, he said, "Don't kick up a fuss about the cheque. If you do, you know what'll happen . . ." I knew what would happen. I'd heard horror stories from other mothers. They would come back, turn the place upside down, stab me . . . And anyway I couldn't lodge a complaint without reporting Laure . . . I had a peephole and extra locks installed . . . I wonder how I could have lived so long in that state of terror . . .

'No one called me any more, except for a few mothers. They were in the same state as I was . . . Each of us had a network of first names and phone numbers. The phone would ring. I could tell by the voice that it was a mother. It would sound rather timorous, apologetic: "Hello, is this where Laure lives?"

' "Yes."

' "You haven't seen Bruno by any chance?"

' "No, there's no one here right now."

' "Is Laure there? May I speak to her?"

' "No, she's not here. I haven't seen her in two days."

' "They're awful!"

' "Yes, they are awful."

'They would often cry, and so would I. We never said anything more than that . . . Twice I had a father on the line; one of them asked me to tell his son, if I saw him, that he'd get a good hiding if he ever turned up at home, and the other one was like me, lost, and he cried . . . There were two types of parents: those that wanted absolutely nothing more to do with their children, and the others, like me, who were trying desperately to help them. Both methods achieved the same results . . .

'What I was going through with Laure was awful . . . But what I was going through with myself was worse . . .'

She set the pages down on her lap and looked up at me. I found her gaze disturbing, and wondered what she saw in my eyes. I hadn't been listening to her read; I had been looking at her thick curly hair (which is rare among blondes). She had a magnificent head of hair. I'd also been looking at her long, strong thighs; she was wearing trousers that day. I felt as if I had been caught *in flagrante delicto*, committing incest or rape, so I immediately started talking: 'I don't like it when people read aloud.'

'Why not?'

'Because what's meant to be read shouldn't be spoken.'

'But these passages were spoken on the tape – they weren't written . . . Perhaps I read badly.'

'On the contrary, you read very well.'

'Listening helps me to make sense of it all. I only understand now, as I read, the way you've condensed it, what my desires were as I spoke all alone . . . You do a good job . . . Are you finding it interesting?'

'I'm interested.'

'Because of your friend who died?'

'Not just that.'

'Did you love her? Were you in love with her?'

'I made love with her . . . I don't know what being in love means any more.'

'Why not?'

'I think, now, that love has aspects I know nothing about.'

'How old are you?'

'I'll be thirty-six soon.'

'Sometimes very young children have an emotional maturity that many adults don't have. They have an intelligence and generosity towards the object of their love that most adults don't have. You might even say that people lose the ability to love as they grow older.'

'Why do you say that? Do you find me childish? Or rather too old, perhaps?'

'I wasn't thinking of you. I was thinking of the phenomenon of love in general.'

She read the following pages carefully, stopping at certain passages. It was the continuation of the description of Professor Greffier.

'I'd forgotten about writing all that . . . While I was waiting for your next section, I wrote some more pages. I think they'll fit in nicely here, after these. I made a copy. I'm a little wary of you after all . . . When we see each other again you can tell me what you think.'

'You've written other things on Professor Greffier. Do you want me to send you a photocopy?'

A small war was being waged: she wanted to make me responsible for something that she couldn't accept from herself.

'No, I like being surprised at our meetings. When shall we see each other again?'

'Next week, as usual. If I've finished ahead of time, I'll call you.'

'Call me anyway, to tell me what you think of the pages I've just given you. They're about Laure. I think it would be a good idea to put them in at this point.'

'All right, then. See you soon.'

Professor Greffier (continued)

My parents were ordinary shopkeepers and although the shop kept them busy, they were not indifferent to what happened elsewhere – quite the contrary. My father subscribed to *Science et Vie* and my mother to *Historia*. They read. They went to all the shows on the Barret tours and discussed them for days and days afterward. They never missed a concert. They sang in the church choir, although they were not great believers, simply because they liked music. We had a piano and a record-player at home. I wasn't an ignorant child.

When I went to university, I had had a solid middle-class education. And yet I felt I was discovering all sorts of things; I was enchanted. I was elated with what I learnt about the human brain – that highly precise and highly uncertain piece of machinery. I felt as though I was on an archaeological site full of buried treasures: the perfection of neurons, the imperfection of transmissions between them, the space for dreams or nightmares that is called the synapse . . .

And then I met Professor Greffier. As far as I could see, his speciality was a man's field to which I was not admitted because I was a woman. It was that simple: 'Women understand nothing about mechanics.' And since I was not at all drawn to mechanics, I never tried to prove the statement wrong. It was words that forced open the doors of the mechanical universe for me. At the same time, I discovered that being a woman had an important effect on my work and my beliefs.

I met Professor Greffier through a small notice posted in the university lobby: 'Replacement wanted for easy secretarial work. Some typing required. Pay minimal. Call Monique 252–89–23.'

I met Monique. She thought I could do the job and gave me the professor's address and telephone number, saying, 'You'll see, he's a scientist, a thermodynamicist, you know the type . . . He's a bit odd, but not too much trouble.'

She was right about his being 'a bit odd', with his cats, but he was no trouble at all about schedules.

His basic secretarial work was done by the university department and his lab. My job was to take care of his private mail, insurance problems (he was a terrible driver, forever having accidents), and other odds and ends, and type up the final draft of the articles he wrote for popular science magazines. The articles paid well, but he didn't feel they were worthy of his attention . . . He didn't pay me much at all, but it was steady work and I was free to do it whenever

I wanted, as long as I did it on time, which meant that I could be at home with Laure more often. I didn't have to run around as I had before to find small temporary jobs.

If I hadn't become interested in his work, it could have gone on like that until I finished studying, and then ended.

But in the welter of scientific terms that filled his papers, amongst the descriptions of all sorts of motors, all sorts of incomprehensible energy devices, some words held my attention: heat, temperature, order, disorder, energy, friction, cooling, work . . . These same words popped up in my psychology textbooks and in my courses on the physiology of the nervous system.

When he gave me an article to type, he usually said: 'This is my latest fantasy, Luce. Tidy it up, will you?' He called me Luce, pretending he couldn't remember my name. At first I would correct him and remind him my name was Elsa, but to no effect. Then I realised that in naming me Luce, he was appropriating me: I was Luce to him alone. I let him, and became his Luce. It didn't bother me. I was 'the secretary, Luce, who takes care of my paperwork,' just as in some mansions the upstairs maid is called Louise and the cook Marie, no matter what their real names might be.

He lived on the fifth floor of a building that had been modern thirty years earlier. I often took the lift with a blind couple who lived on the third floor. They spent a great deal of time in the lobby of the building waiting for someone to go up in the lift, since it didn't work well and often stopped between floors. They stood patiently, resignedly, motionless, before the door to the contraption. Not knowing if whoever had just come in was familiar with their problem, they would trot out their request for help in voices close to a whisper. They made an impression on me. I thought they were ugly; they sweated a lot, even in winter, and they smelt of onions. Because of them and the dilapidated lift, I felt in the beginning as if to get to Professor Greffier's I had to cross the River Styx, that I was ascending into hell instead of descending, that I was a sort of Charon.

I would ring the doorbell. Often he wasn't in. If he didn't answer, I would let myself in with the key he had given me.

I would go to the office, which was also a bedroom – at least there was a bed in there that was always unmade.

At first I would take advantage of his absence and leave with the work to be done. Later I would stay – I liked being there. I would go through his books. I learnt about thermodynamics on my own. I discovered a universe of which I understood nothing but which attracted me all the same.

Once I had my degrees, and got my first full-time position, it didn't occur to me to give notice. He was fifty-three years old, and I was twenty-six; Laure was six. She had just started going to the local primary school.

I was enjoying myself. What I had learnt at university and what I was learning from Professor Greffier made life seem so fascinating – there were treasures everywhere!

Above my desk at home, I had pinned up passages and definitions that I looked at often, that made me dream:

AFFECT: According to Freud, each instinct expresses itself in terms of affect and in terms of ideas (*Verstellungen*). The affect is the qualitative expression of the quantity of instinctual energy and of its fluctuations . . . (Laplanche and Pontalis, *The Language of Psycho-Analysis*)

QUOTA OF AFFECT: A quantitative factor postulated as the substratum of the affect as this is experienced subjectively. The 'quota of affect' is the element that remains invariable despite the various modifications which the affect undergoes . . . (Laplanche and Pontalis, ibid.)

DISCRETE: *Math.*: Taking on or having a finite or countably infinite number of values: not mathematically continuous.
   Ling. Semiol.: Having definable boundaries, with no gradation or continuity between elements. *Discrete unit*: One of a finite number of segments of the continuous stream that is speech.

Quantal physics, therefore, no longer leads to an objective description of the external world, conformable – in a way instinctive – to the ideal of classical physics; it no longer furnishes anything but a relation between the state of the external world and the knowledge of each observer, a relation which no longer depends solely on the external world itself, but also on the observations and the measurements made by the observer. (L. de Broglie, *Physics and Microphysics*)

The essential physical discontinuity that we now call the quantum of action is practically impossible for us to represent exactly as it really is, because it links the configuration of mechanical systems in space and their dynamic evolution in time in a way that is completely contrary to our intuition and usual ways of thinking, yet its fundamental importance in nature cannot be doubted . . . (L. de Broglie, *Physique et microphysique*)

ZERO: Starting point. Nil; nothing.

ABSOLUTE ZERO: Temperature at which the particles whose motion constitutes heat would have least possible energy (−273.15°C).

Absolute zero . . . The zero which is not zero, yet which is absolute. I dreamt of what −273.16°C might be like, when the cells are paralysed by cold, or −273.14°C, just before total immobility, when there is still a hundredth of a degree of hope . . . Life and death.

Words became a shelter erected around me, a tent made of cloth with a strange but sturdy warp – very sturdy, increasingly sturdy. Certain words, a few words, mixed together, joined together, then moved apart, only to meet up again later and take off again. Atomised words whose liberated particles zigzagged, obstinately following unpredictable courses, wild courses, during which, instead of losing their meaning, they became enriched by other meanings. Instead of incoherence this explosion of words created a luminous coherence: the dazzling universe of knowledge.

I worked alone. It was at a time when the professor's looks still revolted me, and in any case I had soon realised that he had absolutely no interest in teaching. I didn't try to get the least explanation from him. I organised my knowledge in my own way.

Words enabled me to establish a parallel between the mechanisms of the human nervous system and those of any machine. I found that the laws of thermodynamics could be applied, word for word, to the human machine . . . As soon as heat is transferred from one system to another, energy is created; at the same time entropy, or disorder, must occur. The energy and disorder cause changes in the systems. This is just as true for a connecting rod and a valve as it is for two neurons . . . As the system improves and becomes more complex, the disorder grows. In other words, the more order is imposed, the more disorder is created. The more bolts, welds, elbows, by-passes, transmissions or junctions there are, the more energy is lost; the more advanced the machine, the more serious its failures. The more contacts there are, the more entropy. The more laws, rules, parents, food, furniture, houses, schools, climates, the more difficult to maintain mental equilibrium. Child's play! How obvious!

I always tended to see coherence everywhere and the idea of making coherence fit into incoherence or vice versa fascinated me more than anything else. Mental disorder was an order unto itself. All one had to do was to discover the friction, the clashes, the strain, the scribbling . . . It was a piece of cake. All I had to do was develop a method that would allow me to follow the changes in temperature and locate points where heating and cooling occurred . . .

If I hadn't been working alone, I would have immediately been pulled up short by the multiplicity of points of friction in the human machine, and above all by their mysteries. But in the beginning, I didn't even think about enzymes, hormones, chemistry; I saw only a system of pulleys and levers, nothing more than a simple machine. And it hung together! I was a true child of the nineteenth century: everything could be understood.

Then I began to study endocrinology, social psychology, modern architecture, the way social security works. Anything and everything. In fact, anything that even remotely influences people's psyche, modifies it. It still hung together;

it was still consistent with the first law of thermodynamics, which told me that within a given system, energy remains constant, that energy can never be taken away or added.

Here was a perfect organisation infinitely superior to my understanding, but not foreign to it, one which my mind could seize. An eiderdown, in short – nice and warm, nice and soft – in which I wrapped myself. Until the problem with Laure. Until heroin came into the picture. Until I met up with that symbol: the white stuff of absolute disorder, the injection of pure entropy . . . My world was annihilated!

*

(Pages added by Elsa after our last meeting)

I have a hard time talking about Professor Greffier. I would rather write about him. I'm aware of the fact that I can talk about drugs, about Laure as a drug addict (I did it throughout the interviews on which you based the one hundred and forty-three pages, and I did it afterwards, alone, with the tape recorder), but I can't bring myself to do it about my own private life.

I must find the courage to speak to you about my private life, my inner life. But for the time being I can't, so I'm writing.

Professor Greffier didn't teach me a thing; to him I was practical and cheap. Later I became useful, because of what I learnt without his knowing and because of my growing interest in his work.

The man was not in this world, he was in his own world, and then only as a spectator.

He made discoveries without knowing what he was discovering; he understood without understanding. To him, knowledge was the manure that fertilised his instincts and kept his impulses in check. It was acquired once and for all, and it didn't reassure him. He had no need of reassurances. He did not enjoy the comfort of knowledge; he knew only how to live in discomfort. He looked for points of reference only in the unknown; the known did not interest him. He may have been a genius.

131

I was drawn to this adventurer of the laboratory, this explorer of chaos. I was seduced by his ugliness, his deformity.

I must broach the subject of my sexuality, for I admit that it's a bit strange. Generally sexuality involves another, the other, a difference; I, however, experience it in solitude. Not because of modesty, laws, customs, upbringing, shame, or vice, but because it embodies something that cannot be shared, it embodies something that used to be called soul. I can't find another word for it – something unique, whole, that can belong only to one person; something discrete, a discrete value. My sexuality is simple; I have orgasms easily, and not just through the sexual act itself. I climax from curiosity, observation, contemplation, movement; that is, looking, observing, contemplating, and moving give me feelings that enrapture my mind and make me wet. And even if it is a human being who makes me feel this rapture, I enjoy it in absolute solitude; I don't wish to share it and I don't wish it to be otherwise. To me orgasm has nothing to do with the genitals, even though it occurs through them.

I wonder what my sexuality would be like today if I hadn't been widowed. My widowhood protected me from conjugality. I don't think that I could ever have lived a married life. After Jacques died I sought company, support and protection in my studies. I never thought of another man. I continued to live with Jacques. He was dead, and I was living, but we watched Laure grow up together, we studied together, we looked after our money together. He was there. He was more than a spectator; he acted with me. It wasn't sad; it was a partnership. I was both him and me, always. It took me a long time to forget him. In fact, I haven't really forgotten him; my life has absorbed his absence.

A dead man is convenient, but oppressive, too. I'm always afraid of being unfaithful to his spirit. I knew him so little.

This absorption occurred easily, so easily and so happily that I never realised Laure missed her father. We talked about him a lot, and we still do. I wasn't aware that she missed him. And yet . . .

And yet I should mention two things I left out when telling you about Laure in the interviews you used for the one hundred and forty-three pages. They were not involuntary lapses; on the contrary, they were facts that I purposely censored. In writing them down now I realise that they are tied to my own sexuality. I have used the third person. The first person singular seemed far too restrictive for writing about it.

Laure's Flat

Laure was nineteen when she started film school, and she had only one idea in mind: to live alone, to have her own place, to leave Elsa. But she didn't know how to say it; she was afraid that her mother would take it the wrong way, that she would see it as a slight, that she would be hurt. Laure didn't want to hurt her mother for anything in the world, so she didn't express her desire, but it grew, burdening her, and then one night it exploded.

That night she had come in very late and unintentionally awoken Elsa. She had been annoyed at herself for it and at seeing her mother up, sleepy-eyed, dishevelled, worried. Suddenly she just blurted out: 'Elsa, I can share almost everything with you, but not absolutely everything. I simply don't want to . . . For example, the friends I just spent the evening with . . . Merely thinking about the face you would make if you saw them makes me abandon the idea . . . I don't bring them home, so I see them in bars. Or not even in bars, 'cause they haven't any money . . . I see them in the street, anywhere at all . . . Straight away that makes them more important than they probably are. And more than anything else, it creates a bad relationship between us . . . I'm not used to hiding things from you, fibbing to you like a little kid . . . I can't stand doing that . . . You're a psychologist – you know I have my own life to live. It's nothing extraordinary. No reason for you to get up and make faces as if it were the end of the world . . . I can't stand not getting along with you, and I can't stand acting like a well-brought-up little girl . . . And I certainly can't stand seeing how emotionally dependent I am on you . . . If I had my own flat, just one or two rooms, I could solve the problem. There wouldn't be a problem. Do you understand?'

A real break, the first. Laure's outburst, gentle but direct, marked an abrupt end to the path they had been following, clutching each other tightly, for almost twenty years.

At the time, Laure had thought that Elsa took it badly, but after a short silence, her mother had looked at her affectionately: 'What's so special about these friends of yours?'

'I don't know. They're kind of weird, you know, kind of bums, kind of . . .'

'Film school friends?'

'Not really. More like . . . Around the school, around film, all that. I'm not really in the mood to tell you about them right now.'

Laure had always done what she had to do. She had learnt long ago how to organise her time to prepare for examinations, dance, do sports, how to arrange things so that none of her activities interfered with any of the others. 'I don't know anyone as well-balanced as my daughter,' Elsa would say admiringly. At the same age, Elsa would have been unable to run her life so self-assuredly.

That's how the idea of the flat came about. Elsa's savings and a recent inheritance from her old aunt in Marseilles had added up to a nice little nest-egg, so why not?

Buying two maid's rooms in the fifteenth *arrondissement*, fixing them up and moving Laure in was no small task. It took at least three months for them to cut the cord definitively. At first, claiming that her room smelt of paint, Laure would go home and sleep at her mother's almost every night. But in the end they adjusted to the change of pace. They saw or called each other every day. Elsa never went over to her daughter's without being invited. She had promised herself that she wouldn't from the beginning and she kept that promise.

Laure observed her mother from afar, affectionate and worried. At the least sign of distress she would have gone back.

Once she was alone at home, Elsa had taken over her daughter's room, storing her papers there, and setting up her secretary, who had used to work in the sitting room. She went at it almost with a vengeance.

Laure thought it was to deny her absence, to fill the void, so that she wouldn't suffer from it. More than once it wrung her heart to think of Elsa's solitude. Until one day she realised that her mother was fine, that she was really doing very well. It was around then that Elsa had met François at a conference. She had talked about her affair with a nonchalance and gaiety that Laure had never seen in her before.

Laure was quite proud of the way it had all worked out. She had blown apart the structure that had been suffocating them. She had destroyed it completely and she had been right to do so, because Elsa, unaware of the cocoon she had spun for herself, would have continued in the same way for ages, perhaps forever.

Elsa had brought Laure into the world and now Laure was bringing Elsa into the world. Elsa, the famous psychologist, the expert!

They had talked about this metamorphosis.

'Elsa, you're looking younger and more beautiful every day. And you're doing more than you've ever done before. Do you realise how you've changed?'

'Of course. I've never felt better.'

'So what do you put it down to?'

'To tell you the truth, I don't really want to know. I'd rather practise psychology on other people than on myself.'

'You're in love, that's what it is.'

'Oh, my affair with François doesn't take up a lot of time. We rarely see each other. It's fun having a lover, but he isn't the centre of my life. He's on the other side of the Atlantic . . . I don't think men have ever really meant much to me . . . Or maybe I've never really given myself the time to let them.'

'What about your old professor?'

'He's resigned himself to it.'

'Then it's because I'm out of your way now that you're getting on so well?'

'You'll never be out of my way, my sweet, my dearest, my darling daughter, my Lo Lo, my little doll.'

And they were off laughing, showering each other with terms of endearment, playing the games they had invented, of which they never seemed to tire.

In the last year Elsa had travelled a great deal; she had attended several conferences. And she had worked hard preparing a paper for publication that meant a great deal to her. Laure, too, was busy with some sort of project or other that seemed to occupy a lot of her time. Elsa thought she looked peaky.

'You're doing too much, Laure dear.'

'Elsa, please don't start going all maternal on me.'

Laure's Dreams

When she was a child, Laure told Elsa all her dreams. That was how they spent the better part of every Sunday morning, the only day they both had the time for it. During the week, in the kitchen, because she was afraid of being late for school, Laure would say as she wolfed down her breakfast: 'What a dream I had last night . . . I'll tell you all about it on Sunday.' And Elsa would remind her, 'Be sure to remember it, now. Dreams are important.'

The dreams were often about exotic modern wars. The landscape looked like the Pacific islands or Vietnam, the way it was in films or on TV. It was hot. There were a lot of people, speaking all sorts of languages. There were markets selling strange, attractive fruits and flowers. The women were half-naked, languorous, wet with perspiration. The men were dressed in either uniforms or rags. Elsa was holding her firmly by the hand and they were making their way through the crowd. Neither of them was afraid of anything, and yet it was dangerous. There was danger in the air. Laure liked being there; she liked to feel her heart pounding; she liked to have people looking at her. A soldier looked at her, a tall blond soldier in camouflage uniform, a hero. He kept staring at her. She would wake up in a sweat, wanting to return to the dream but never managing to.

Sometimes the wars were archaic cosmic wars on another planet. The Earth was very far away, multi-coloured, round, but that didn't matter, since the planet they were on was just as pleasant. Yet Elsa said that there were diplodocus and octopus, that they had already eaten someone alive, and that she and Laure had to leave. Unknown to her mother, Laure went off to look for the monsters. She discovered a dry, dusty place, a huge geographic area, an infinite confusion of rocky hills. There, slimy animals were gorging themselves on the body of a man who kept on dying. Through some fantastic process, he kept being reborn from his own blood, shredded flesh, spilled viscera, shattered limbs. The creatures, mere viscous heaps, were totally absorbed in feeding off this inexhaustible body. Laure, reassured, ran off to tell Elsa that there was no danger, but she knew that it would serve no purpose, that her mother would leave in any case.

Elsa was good at helping her interpret these stories of wars, monsters, the hero in the shadow, the inexhaustible corpse. They were all her father. She was proud of him. She counted herself lucky to have a father like that, young, handsome, killed at war. She didn't miss him. In Laure's mind, Jacques was always linked to the warmth of Elsa's bed on Sunday morning.

When she began to take an interest in boys, little by little, she stopped telling Elsa about her dreams. Her mother knew too much about her, and she needed to have some secrets. She needed some form of escape . . . Laure's problem was that throughout her adolescence she had to unlearn the habits she had acquired in childhood, like her habit of always telling everything to Elsa, not just her dreams or worries, but also her successes.

Elsa, Elsa, Elsa, always Elsa . . . Always the same old story!

People who had known Jacques said that Laure was very like him. She couldn't remember him. She knew only what other people told her, and of course, what she imagined.

The year she turned thirteen, she got her period, and on

that day Elsa offered to let her read the letters that Jacques had sent during the war, as if they would make her a woman the same way her blood did.

Why had Elsa done that?

Laure read the letters over and over again until they no longer held any meaning, until they were nothing but scribbles on paper. Then the paper itself began to take on meaning. She would put the letters on the table, stretch out on her bed and stare at them. Into them she would read a foreign country, danger, her father's rage at the time of his death. And then even the paper lost its meaning. All that was left was her father's inability to come to terms with his own refusal, his refusal to wage war. Not even that; all that was left was the desire to leave. Elsewhere, wherever it was different, there, on the table.

Laure only took out the letters when her mother wasn't home. At first, despite the fact that Elsa had already given her permission, she did it secretly. She would put them back exactly where they had been, in the order she had found them. She thought that her mother read them often. Once, caught unawares when Elsa returned earlier than expected, she hid them under her mattress. Several days passed before she could slip them back into the folder where they were kept. The whole time, they had weighed upon her mind like an unconfessed sin. Fortunately Elsa had never noticed a thing. It happened again several times. Laure eventually realised that her mother didn't look at the letters, so she kept them in her room, she appropriated them. The folder in Elsa's office remained empty. When she moved into her own flat, Laure took the letters with her. By that time she had long since decided that Elsa no longer loved Jacques and that perhaps she never had. Thus, through a sort of deceit that wasn't really deceit, the letters had changed addressee: now they were addressed to Laure, and they held history lessons, lessons in which Jacques taught Laure that history was incomplete because it didn't tell his story, the story of his refusal.

Laure was always elegant, dressed to the nines, pressing the pleats of her trousers before going to school. She was the most beautiful girl, and she grew more beautiful all the time. Her teachers were drawn to her, the traffic policeman was drawn to her, the shopkeepers were drawn to her, her mother was drawn to her. And then came a time – she was about fifteen – when she realised that a great deal of her success depended on her beauty, and from that point on she changed. She began systematically to defend the cause of the oppressed. She decided she wanted to study law; she felt that the look of others was a form of oppression. She wanted to fight against it, she wanted to free humanity from it. She could not accept the fact that one's appearance could have a greater effect on one's destiny than one's intelligence did. From then on she was interested in people on the fringes, and decided to study film instead of law. She wanted to use images differently, change perceptions . . . She started taking less care of herself. She still had the same grace and she knew it, but she only allowed it free rein with Elsa. It was a privilege she granted only her mother, for murky reasons neither of them sought to understand.

For close to six months now I haven't done a thing. I haven't seen anyone but Elsa. And I don't think those meetings, dropping off my copy like a diligent pupil, can really be called seeing her. I hear about nothing but passion, write about nothing but passion, read about nothing but passion, experience nothing but passion, but I never make love and I never say I love you. I can't stand it any more.

I'm going to abandon this project, tell her I can't live life the way she does: with unceasing, unremitting passion. That's what I tell myself when I turn off the tape recorder, and ten minutes later I turn it on again, and listen to it – to her – and it starts all over.

I'm like her; I no longer know what I'm doing.

At the beginning of the session following the one where she had given me *Laure's Dreams* and *Laure's Flat*, she acted very defensively, trying to justify herself. She started by making categorical judgments and stating eternal truths with authority, which was not her usual style. She sounded like someone pleading not guilty, but not convinced of her own innocence. She launched into a real speech. It seemed to me that for the first time she was discovering herself.

'The time has come to reflect upon what my real relationship with my daughter must have been and to conclude that it was the reason she became addicted to heroin . . . But that would be too simplistic.

'Why did I "forget" to talk about Laure's dreams and her flat?'

'Why did I enjoy my freedom so much after she left?'

'Why did I give her her father's letters on the day she menstruated for the first time?'

I said nothing.

'Mothers' guilt spoils everybody's lives; their own first of all, then that of their children, of their men, and of everyone else around them into the bargain.

'A woman rarely hurts her child on purpose . . . If a

woman is found guilty because of her unconscious actions, then everything that went into making her must be judged, starting with her own parents, and her parents' parents, and society since time immemorial . . . Everyone knows that! It's like proving the existence of God: the best proof that God does not exist is that one has to look for proof of his existence . . . Mothers are not guilty!

'I'm getting angry. I'm sorry, it's stupid of me, but I find it unacceptable that mothers should be blamed for most of society's ills. Delinquents, the mentally disturbed, drug addicts, alcoholics – they all had mothers who were too much like this or not enough like that! . . . The sins of mothers clutter up our newspapers and television screens. Mothers are good only when they are cancelled out by their sacrifices . . . It would be a much better idea to try to understand how mothers became mums . . . little by little, in scarcely a century! No one listened to me when I wrote and said that. They said I was a feminist! That's ridiculous, I detest ghettos. It's a sociological phenomenon, an economic phenomenon! . . . Mums are one of the monstrosities of modern times . . .

'I have always tried to make sure the mothers of the children I was treating didn't feel guilty. Mothers are entitled to their own lives!

'Mothers' guilt entered our morality at the same time as Freud was popularised. Freud himself would have been better off not theorising on his flashes of genius. In theorising, he fell into every trap he spoke out against. For every word he wrote, he has to be psychoanalysed. For every word, one has to remember that he was a man, a Jew, an Austrian, a product of the nineteenth century, and that he only treated the middle class . . . It's tiresome.

'And yet I would be lying if I said that I never thought about my guilt during the three years of wandering . . . I've thought about it a lot and often. Have I already talked to you about my guilt?'

'No, not really.'

'Nor about my sexuality . . . I never really had problems with my sexuality. These days, that probably seems odd . . .'

'Professor Greffier . . .'

'Oh him! From what I can see, I've talked about him in the new pages as well.'

'Yes, a great deal.'

'What do you think about it?'

'I never imagined that a man and a woman could have a relationship like that . . . This penis like a periscope, like a truncheon . . .'

'We can take all that out.'

'I don't think we should. We have to go all the way.'

'Does it really bother you when I read aloud?'

'No. The other day I wasn't happy with what I'd written. I didn't think the pages you were reading were very good.'

'There are a lot today. Would you like to make yourself more comfortable, take off your jacket? Would you like some coffee or anything else to drink?'

'No thanks, I'm fine.'

She began to read:

'Before I wound up in Professor Greffier's bed – the one in his office that was always unmade – I met quite a few men, bachelors. (I'm afraid to get in between a couple, no matter what state their relationship is in. Couples . . .) It never crossed my mind to live with any of them. They were only of fleeting importance to me. They added some fun to my life, diversion, lightened it up. I never invited them home, and Laure never met them. I'm still friends with some of them.

'So one day I had sex with him. It was bound to happen. It happened with every woman he knew. I knew that it would happen with me, too. It was inevitable.

'And yet he did nothing for it: he didn't court me, he never made insinuations, but he subtly became more intimate with me. He became freer in the way he behaved, spoke, moved; he wasn't just casual, he was familiar. Yes, that's it, he became familiar with me although I had no personal relationship with him. While the forms of address he used were still polite and respectful, his tone, his voice became increasingly familiar; it was the intimate tone of sexual relations – and I was well aware of it. I let him, as I had let him call me Luce. It amused me more than anything else. I thought that perhaps that was how men of his generation went about seducing a woman. He was both very immediate and yet indifferent. If anything happened between us it was important, and then again it wasn't.

'In thermodynamics, time is a fundamental and irreversible value. As time passes, a working system must change, because entropy must increase. To Professor Greffier, who spent his time with time, the Luce system that had just been linked to his own could only evolve into increasing disorder. One day, because the systems had entered into a relationship, Luce would either slam the door in his face or get into his bed, in which case he would be able to study Luce's entropy at home. It might take some time, but it was an experiment like any other, and I lent myself to it without fear. I thought that I could control Luce, dominate her.

'There were notebooks all over his desk. Most of them contained notes on his experiments in progress. Figures, letters, equations, mixed up with short sentences. But some of them contained annotations on people, who were always referred to by initials. Only women. For example, "S nice dress. Flirtatious. Bed. Dirty-minded. Then furious: 'Bastard! Cock like a fish-hook! Always angling for another catch!' " or "F distraught. Crazy over affair with S because of N's gossip. 'You get another woman pregnant and I'll kill her!' Slammed door. Phone rang all night." etc. Notes on extremely violent outbursts, wild, lubricious, jealous, salacious women, all in telegraphic style. On his own reactions throughout these tempests, there was nothing. A victim. I felt sorry for him . . . The phone rang often. He asked me not to answer it when he was out, and when he was there, he replied with just a word or two, gently: "Right . . . Of course . . . Certainly not . . . Don't worry." Sometimes I could hear vociferous protests from the other end of the line. Then I would look at him, and he would shut his eyes as if in pain, place the receiver on his chest, and wait for it to pass. A martyr. Afterwards, as after his fights with the cats, he would sit down beside me to work, and we would never mention it.

'I waited for the physical revulsion I felt for him to disappear. Little by little, it did diminish, and in its place grew an affection I still feel. He was a repugnant man, yet at the same time he inspired sympathy. There was something of the child in him. He was a huge mass of hopes and desires that failures or setbacks never made a dent in.

'There were two sides to him: he was both actor and acted upon. My fits of anger, fired by the discovery of his calculated self-interest, ebbed in the face of his innocence. The exact same principle of work is central to thermodynamics: for work to be produced, there must be a transfer of heat between two bodies . . . Always two and always heat . . .

'With him, I lived in a state of ambiguity I never suspected could be experienced. We were bound by ties of which we were unaware. We each situated our relationship on terrain the other did not suspect. He was interested in tomorrow, what comes next, afterwards. When would the machine go out of control? Would it break down? To me, space was more important than time. The mind, with the memory as a floodlight, sweeps across time, lights up the past. The past can become present in the mind's duration.

'He never took any account of me, nor what my life had been before I knew him, nor what it was like now outside of his office. The only thing he took into account was Luce. In short, we mixed my space and his time in an absurd but very efficient match, because we worked a great deal, both together (I continued to the end to "tidy up" his articles and later, even his research papers), and separately throughout the time our relationship lasted. He had absolute confidence in my judgment. He couldn't do anything any more without discussing it with me. I often felt as if I had two children: Laure and an infant who could have been my father. It lasted over fifteen years, without my knowing why . . .

'Always the same old thing. Relationships between women and children, women and snakes, over and over again . . . What a bore!

'We split up at the beginning of my experience of heroin with Laure. I still don't know why I decided at that point that Luce was a burden to me. It's true that she was not a part of my family life and that I had every intention of devoting myself solely to that life. But there was more to it than that.

'What made me break with the woman who was Professor Greffier's lover, "the fearsome, dutiful courtesan" (as he called me later in his notes), the hard worker, the disciple, the scientist?

'He couldn't stand my being increasingly captivated by my work, increasingly absent. He couldn't stand anything about me that was not Luce, "his little secretary". He humiliated me, hurt me. He spoke only to Luce, his idea of Luce: a totally uninteresting young woman he had brought up to his own level, a slave. It was impossible to get him away from that. I blamed myself because I could not manage to extricate myself from the rut he had put me into. I blamed myself because I kept going back. I blamed myself because I insisted on showing him that I wasn't the woman he thought I was . . . He couldn't have cared less – the essential thing was that I kept coming back.

'When he found out about François, it became hellish. He said he knew no one but mere crutches, nurses, furies of the lab – I was the only one, the only woman in his life, his woman . . . He made sordid, imbecilic, pathetic scenes . . . The more pathetic it became, the more satisfied he was: he had been right, the Luce machine was just what he had set up, the experiment was going as predicted . . . How could it have lasted so long? Complacency on my part? Masochism? Lucidity? I don't know. I have to try and understand Luce.

'All things considered, it wasn't the ups and downs of Laure's perdition and then salvation that destroyed my equilibrium, though that was hard, very hard, sometimes horrible. I saw Laure's friends, people I knew well, dying of overdoses before my very eyes; I don't know how many times I saw my own daughter come close to death. I lived with the likelihood of Laure's death for three years, day in, day out, hour after hour. More than once I envied mothers whose children died of cancer . . . At least they can talk about it, at least they get some compassion . . . But that illness, that slow death, the death of drug addicts . . . The young bodies tossed aside like rubbish . . . The shame and wrath that accompanies them to the morgue . . . It's appalling . . . And yet that's not what destroyed me. It was something much deeper than that.

'I never used to believe in chance or the devil. I believed in knowledge. I believed that what couldn't be solved today would be solved tomorrow. I believed that knowledge, applied intelligently, could solve anything.

'I built my professional life – actually my entire life – upon that hope. And it crumbled. Heroin conjured up chance and the devil, and I was incapable of putting a halt to the havoc they wreaked.

'Professor Greffier was old, but in a way he was ageless. He was a man so dedicated to matter, to the study of the decay of matter, to the inexorable destruction that generates freshness and newness, that he was indifferent to his body. He never changed. He grew older, of course. I saw him become hunched, flabby, crumpled, wrinkled, but that had no effect on his behaviour. Only numbers made an impression on him. He had seen his sixtieth and seventieth birthdays come and go with a sort of dread. During those years he often said that he was ageing, because he was getting into the next decade, because of the numbers, for no other reason.

'All his time was spent in his lab or at his desk. He stopped at noon for a light meal that he ate without knowing what was on his plate, then had a brief rest and started again. I often observed him while he was at his desk. He wrote out his calculations, his predictions, seeing worlds that he alone could see. His ears would turn red and he would get that faraway look in his eyes: he was inventing. He wore himself out inventing.

'To get through the time that he could not spend at work, he manipulated human machines, puppets whose workings seemed simpler to him than those of his other machines. Invariably, the dolls would explode in his hands, becoming animated with their own energy, transforming order into disorder uncontrollably, and finally disintegrating. Despite the recurrence of these disastrous transformations, he persisted in building a collection of human machines with which he could repeat the same experiment, always asking them to play the same role. To him, these dream creatures were all

146

identical, since they all had a woman's breasts and vulva . . .
He couldn't understand why it didn't work. His innocence
was disarming. He would be genuinely disappointed. He
found satisfaction only in the exile of the world he had created, in his mechanical inventions, and nothing outside that
world really interested him.

'I think I was the only one of his puppets who ever took
an interest in his work. That's probably why our relationship
lasted so long.

'When we saw each other we talked about his work in
progress and made love.

'He had a magnificent penis that was always ready for
action and to which he was quite indifferent. While we made
love he would close his eyes, turning his head – even hiding
his face in a pillow sometimes – and let me do what I wanted.
He gave his superb phallus up to my fantasies and I could
do whatever I wished with it. There was no need to seduce
him, please him, excite him; I had only to satisfy my own
wildest, most obscene, most tender desires . . . When it was
over we would pick up a conversation about his work where
we had left it off.

'In fact, while he was surrendering his penis, while his face
was closed or hidden, he was extremely attentive to the
puppet's fantasies. He was interested the way an entomol-
ogist is interested in an ant or a cockroach. Later, when we
had our scenes, he would use what he had learnt about me
to hurt and subjugate me. It was despicable . . . As he often
mixed up his memories of other women with his memories
of me, I came to realise that the actual number of sexual
fantasies is quite limited. There are only a few variations on
a few themes . . . In the end, sex is "discrete".

'He never asked me to make love; I was always the one
who wanted to. Like other extremely potent men, he never
talked about sex and he never publicly bragged about his
conquests. Sex was for the bedroom alone, for his bed, and
elsewhere there was no question of it. In any case, as the
performance of his organ was never a problem for him, what
he found important in sex was how it revealed character, or
to be more precise, how it revealed what was hidden in
people's characters: vices, pettiness, quirks . . .

'I don't feel capable of writing any more about it. Or else I'd have to write thousands of pages on pride, shame, idiocy and the codification of civilised sexual conduct. And on the beauty of the sex act, the splendours of the orgasm.

'My life was as full as it could be. I had my daughter, my career, that man. I never realised the alienation I was sinking into. How could I? I never had a second to myself to take a step back.

'And then, despite what I have just written, which emphasises the negative side of my relationship with Professor Greffier by separating it from the rest, I must say that generally things were wonderful, and the future looked bright. I had been accepted onto a team doing endocrinological research. Laure had grown up into a young woman. My appointment diary was fully booked months in advance. I thought I was living in the present. I thought I was growing.

'I didn't realise that I was becoming mired in stifling certainties. All those years, I considered temperature to be a thing, because I could measure it. And yet cold and heat are not things.

'When my work was suddenly interrupted by Laure's drug problem, when I saw her boiling or icy depending on whether she needed heroin or not, I thought I would be able to solve the problem easily.

'Yet not only did I not solve it, but all my efforts to understand it seemed vain and useless.

'That's where I am now.'

She stopped. Her gaze was remote. I had seen that expression before, when she was in distress.

'Are you all right?'

'I'm fine, fine . . . Don't you find it indecent?'

'What?'

'Everything I say about Professor Greffier.'

'I wouldn't use the word indecent. I would say shocking, rather.'

'What do you mean?'

'It's shocking that anyone could call that love, making love.'

She stared at me: her eyes took hold of my face and carried it off. Afterward, when our gazes met, I felt I no longer had any expression; it was as if she had decapitated me. I couldn't understand the look she gave me.

She took up the remaining pages and began to read again.

'I still have things to say . . . I have to talk about how Laure kicked the habit. It was no thanks to me. I had nothing to do with it. She did it by herself . . .

'I wanted to avoid lapsing into a confession . . . The idea of sin muddles me . . . Intimate details are of no interest . . . What I've just said is stupid . . . That's exactly why I'm here, facing this tape recorder – to talk about intimate details . . . Intimacy . . . Innermost, in the heart . . . The heart is part of intimacy . . . Sex is part of privacy . . . The heart and sex are two very different things . . . Sex is "discrete". To a physicist, it would be a discontinuous value: it can be isolated and located . . . The heart, on the other hand, is continuous: it cannot be isolated from any of our motivations. Or, if you like, we are only motivated as long as it beats . . . I don't know what I'm getting into here, at the moment . . . It's just occurred to me that the discontinuity of sex when it connects or is connected to the continuum of the heart . . . It's just occurred to me that under those conditions, the way I see it, which is purely speculative, they constitute the soul . . . Those are the times when we have a soul . . . in this relationship . . . in this relativity . . . But none of that means a thing. Or maybe it does mean something . . . I'm tired of reasoning like this . . .

'The heart, all that blood moving around for so long . . . I've often thought that my death would be the only thing to stop the racket it makes . . . I was in such a state of exhaustion . . . I couldn't imagine anything any longer, or hope for anything . . . I no longer wanted to know where I was, what time it was, who I was, or anything. Nothing but extenuated matter. I heard my matter beating, in my face, in my belly, in my hands, in my legs . . . in all the parts of my body that were in contact with something else. And since I didn't want to know that there was anything else, I hated my heart, for it reminded me with each beat that something else existed. I wanted it to stop . . . That blasted pump beats four thousand eight hundred times an hour! It needs a terrific amount of energy to send the blood to the tips of one's toes, through kilometres and kilometres of ducts . . . And the damn machine really holds up well . . . Sticky blood, sweet blood. Stickiness. Stickiness recycled four thousand eight hundred times an hour.

'When I first became aware of Laure's problem, I decided to break off my relationship with the professor. I couldn't go on leading the double affective life I had made for myself: Laure on the one hand, the professor on the other. In any case, I'd lost interest in his work. I found that he was starting to ramble somewhat. By that time, he was essentially nothing more to me than a penis. I'd had enough of his dildo-penis. I blamed myself for not knowing how to resist the temptation of the guaranteed orgasms I experienced with him. I couldn't bring myself to break free of it. And then perhaps, too, in some silly sort of way, I didn't want to relinquish the magnificent instrument to another woman; over the years, I had become its sole user . . . In any case, from the day I told him I was leaving, I was in a constant state of anxiety. I felt as if I had lost my life-jacket, my buoy . . . I've only recently begun to realise that it was not the loss of his member (what a word!) that distressed me, but something else . . . I don't know exactly what . . .

'I didn't have time to think about it during the three years of perdition – I was warding off distress with reasoning along the lines of "plenty of other fish in the sea", and I would find another man when I had the time . . . I attributed my anxiety entirely to what I was going through with Laure. It was afterwards, only afterwards, that I tried to discover the truth and became completely lost.

'I must say that the way that Laure gave up drugs was an even bigger enigma to me than her inability to do so for over three years.

'One day she took off with Adrian, a drug addict even more addicted than she was, if that's possible. They went to stay with some friends of mine who lived in an out-of-the-way spot; the nearest village was kilometres away. These friends had known Laure for a long time and were very fond of her. They had no idea what was going on. They saw her and her friend arrive, both ill. They put them up in a building that they usually let in the summer. Laure got word to me that that was where she was.

'She and Adrian stayed there for six months.

'Experts claim that two drug addicts can never kick the habit together, that one of them will always drag the other one down again. But they did it . . .

'To help them stop, they had the usual prescriptions, provided by my friend in Marseilles. We had tried others and had always come back to those. Adrian had a few methadone pills. Methadone is just as addictive as heroin, and they knew that. The day they arrived they went and hid them, well wrapped in a plastic bag, under a big stone a good distance from the house where they were staying, about five hundred metres. They knew that soon withdrawal would make going five hundred metres in the cold and rain – they were in moorland where it's always raining – a tremendous effort . . . In the end they never went; the pills must still be there.

'I visited them three times, for about two weeks each time.

'They lived like that, in that alienation, that solitude, that dampness, unable to do anything but cling to their desire to get off drugs, obstinate, in pain, turned in on their withdrawal, observing it, probing it, assessing it, for days on end. They spent the first few days without sleeping, intensely strung-out. They endured the torture of that insomnia. And then they slept a few hours each night. During those hours, they had dreams about drugs, nightmares that they told each other, shivering before the peat fire that gave off hardly any heat. They were at that stage when I visited them for the first time. They both had the same dream: they were fixing themselves a good hit, lovingly warming the liquid, drawing it into the syringe. They would tie up, slide the needle into the bulging vein in the crook of the arm, and then, just as they were about to push the plunger in, they would wake up with a start! When Laure had finished telling her dream, Adrian would tell his, or vice versa: the details of their dreams were always the same. Their subconscious had been invaded and made uniform by drugs. They were like identical twins in many other ways as well: they had the same likes, the same dislikes; they used the same images, the same words. There was absolute complicity between the two of them, built entirely around drugs. That was their world; they had no other. They were in a prison, under the tight surveillance of dope. I watched these sessions transfixed, wondering how long they would be able to resist the temptation to return to Paris, or to fetch the methadone. I never thought they would hold out. I thought they would crawl through the mud to the big stone, on their stomachs if they had to.

'Once a week they went with their hosts to buy groceries. Laure knew the dangers of alcohol and never bought any. Adrian bought a little beer, but she didn't touch it. They had next to no money. They cooked soups and pasta. When I was there, we feasted on steak, grains, fish, cakes. Their bodies, deprived of heroin, would give them no peace. Laure had one bout of bronchitis after another, and she menstruated constantly with dreadful cramps. Adrian's teeth were in a terrible state. His gums were swollen with abscesses. They knew that their health problems were real and that they would have no trouble getting tranquillisers, even powerful ones, legally; the village doctor would have innocently pre-scribed them. But they resisted. They made do with aspirin, antibiotics, broth and extract of cloves . . . Laure told me that withdrawal was not as bad this time as the other times. Coming down had been hard, but incomparably easier than before. What was the explanation? . . .

'After three months – three months! – of staying holed up, they started to take some exercise: fetching peat, cleaning the house, visiting their hosts on the other side of the river. The methadone had become accessible, but they never considered digging it up. They talked about it, thumbed their nose at it, made fun of it. From one of the windows of the house they could see the big stone in the distance.

'Adrian said, "It takes six months for the liver and kidneys to begin to function more or less normally again. After that we plan to go back to Paris." I don't know where he heard that, but the six-month time period became sacred.

'He began to write about his experiences. He was the eldest of a large, extremely poor family. He loved to announce:

"I'm a member of the lumpenproletariat." His father had walked out on them. He wanted to help his mother, whom he adored. He started to do odd jobs, to earn money however he could. He was fifteen at the time. I've seen pictures of him: a tall, intelligent-looking boy, with curly brown hair and very beautiful light eyes. He was easy prey for dealers who skimmed the streams of misery. Like something out of Zola . . . Somebody made him a "mule", a drug courier. Adrian earned more money doing that than he ever had before. So he worked as a "mule" more and more often. He tried dope. It's always the same old story: a few joints to start with, to go along with the crowd, then a little coke, a little H afterwards, snorting first and then shooting up. He became addicted. He met Laure . . . He wrote about all that. Laure helped him write. They loved each other . . . He sent his essay to a well-known weekly. It was accepted and published in two instalments, and he got a good fee for it.

'After six months they came back to Paris. They wanted to live with me, in the shelter of my answering machine, my address, my quiet neighbourhood, my secure building. They set themselves another deadline: two years.

'Adrian became a journalist, and Laure started to make shorts and advertising films. Their work is very interesting.

'While they were out in the country, I tried to start doing something again, but I had to remain available in case their experiment failed. So I didn't take my patients on again. I ran a few workshops, wrote a few articles; I worked part-time for Social Security. That brought me back to my roots. I should have found it interesting, but I didn't. Nothing interested me any more.

'At first I thought that it was because I was tired, that the years of wandering had exhausted me, that it was just a question of a few days, maybe a few weeks. Then I thought it might be due to the fact that I was not really devoting myself entirely to my work, that my mind was elsewhere. Then, when they came back to Paris, when I could see that they were really living again, that they spoke of heroin less and less, when I understood that they had kicked heroin and were hooked on something else – on themselves as a couple first of all, and on their work – I began to founder.

'I saw Professor Greffier again. He looked very old. He was drifting aimlessly at the sad end of his existence. What had kept him going was his work, so he insisted on working, but he no longer discovered anything. He couldn't discover anything because he wasn't looking any more. He went through his old experiments, but he didn't try anything new. He, too, was suffocating. And although he had never led a normal life, he clung to the idea of having a normal life.

'It was abject defeat, the end of our world. We no longer had anything to say to each another. He was retiring, cloaked in his considerable reputation, with his admirable phallus, his skin game, very much alive and well-ensconced in his trousers. I was entering the void.'

'And what's next?'

'Another passage on Professor Greffier.'

'That's going to be too much.'

'As soon as I've tidied it up, I'll post it. I'm going to have a rest.'

'You never mentioned that before.'

'No, I've just decided.'

'Are you tired?'

'I've had enough for the time being, enough of everything.'

'Will I be able to get in touch with you?'

'I don't know where I'm going. I'm just taking my car and leaving. I think the best thing for me would be a change of scenery.'

'Is there anything I can do for you?'

'No. I don't think so, unfortunately . . . I don't know why I said unfortunately . . . I'm a very ordinary person, you know. It's summer, and I need a holiday, like everyone else. That's all there is to it.'

'Am I boring you with my stories?'

'A little.'

'Won't we finish the book?'

'Oh, so you want to do a book now!'

She was discomfited. She looked like a schoolgirl caught misbehaving. The woman made me melt inside . . . Oh no, I wasn't going to start that all over again. I wasn't going to be had a second time. I'd said I was leaving and leave I would.

'Goodbye, then. I'll ring you as soon as I'm back.'

(Pages sent by post 1 August)

Professor Greffier (continued)

There were the three years of drug-taking.

Then there were the six months of kicking, in the country, with the temptation of methadone buried under a big rock.

Then there were the two years of recovery and readjustment in the city.

Five and a half years, during which day by day I sank deeper and deeper into incoherence.

While Laure diced with death, I was concerned only with her macabre gamble. I submitted to the incoherence that had swept over me without analysing it. No rest. Too many emergencies. Too many surprises, shocks, questions, changes, journeys – and too many splendours as well. Drug addicts are incapable of talking about their condition, so they express it through dazzling make-up, superb outfits, amazing combinations of colours, shapes and forms . . . freedom with words, free, funny, serious words, words that speak several languages at once. I had to interpret all that . . . It left me reeling.

Everything seemed to come tumbling down around me. I felt myself to be *terra firma*, solidity, stability. I barricaded myself so I wouldn't be buried. It seemed to me that if I didn't cling to my convictions, my laws, my knowledge, Laure would die. And yet all that was swept away and Laure is still living . . .

When I say that during those years I was stripped of everything, that's not quite true. The gleam and warmth of their eyes are still with me, the black velvet of their pupils dilated by withdrawal, or the brightness of their irises, with their pupils contracted in bliss, irises shining green, blue, or brown, filling the entire space between the eyelids, Modigliani irises. Their eyes would radiate contentment and doubt that reason could not bear. It was as if they knew the essence and had to keep it to themselves. When they were high, there was an unbearable look of trust in their eyes. I sometimes took them for oracles whose words could not be heard, or sacrificial victims on the altars of a demon spirit. I no longer believed in anything, yet those eyes made me want to believe. It was madness! Madness!

I tried to get away, to rescue myself. I wanted to find out what Professor Greffier thought. I saw him several times more. I asked him to receive me in his sitting room, because I didn't want to go into his bedroom. He agreed. But when I arrived, he claimed to be ill . . . blood pressure . . . He hadn't been well and he had to stay on his back, his doctor had recommended it . . . So we ended up in his bedroom, embarrassed to be there like that, bundled up in our clothes, he with his shoes on, me with my handbag on my lap, visiting him.

But the absurdity of the situation actually suited my purpose well in the end. We acted out an interview.

Why was he interested in thermodynamics? What was physics to him?

He didn't know. But since he wanted me to stay and to come back, he tried to find answers. He had first become interested in thermodynamics when he was a student. He had done some training in a lab, and something had captivated him, exactly what, he couldn't say. Something about the subject suited him; it was a labyrinth in which his mind could easily make progress. He enjoyed things others found difficult. He couldn't explain it. There was a path there that was made for him. It was thermodynamics, but it could have been something else. His projects were simple, flowed naturally, and other people found them inspired.

When, in the course of our conversation, I explained to him what thermodynamics had taught me, all that I had been able to imagine about disorder, freedom, time and personality based on thermodynamics, he screwed up his eyes as if what I was saying pained him, as if he didn't want to hear it, and after a while he cut me off: 'I don't like generalities'. It was psychology that he so scornfully called 'generalities'.

'But don't you remember, a long time ago, when instead of answering me when I asked you about entropy, you gave me a book by Charon to read? It's there in your bookcase.'

'I don't remember.'

'I'll show you. It isn't long. I know the page number by heart, page 28. I've read it dozens of times . . . Here, look.'

The word entropy is somewhat similar to the word disorder in its common usage. If we let material elements interact among themselves, the physical laws of the world of matter are such that disorder can only increase. We can, for example, measure the order of a material system by considering the energy that can be extracted from the system. The law of entropy tells us that as time goes by, the possibility of extracting energy from the system decreases because of the continually increasing entropy (disorder) of the system. This holds equally true both for a pot of boiling water which, when removed from the source of heat, can only cool over the course of time, and for a star which, little by little, also cools and eventually dies. In short, we can say that the law of increasing entropy is that which leads everything to its death. Thought, however, has the power to interfere with the 'natural' evolutionary path of matter, somehow to slow down the inexorable progress of matter toward disorder and death, by instilling order that it is capable of 'creating' spontaneously, by taking order from its own psychic substance.

'I have no recollection . . . It must have been centuries ago that I gave you that to read . . . We must have been on very formal terms at that point . . . It was written for the general public. Scientific thought should not be popularised.'

'But you often did it yourself. That's how I started here . . .'

'I do it less and less. And that wasn't the same. I stayed scientific, it was for scientific journals . . . And anyway, that fellow, I forget his name, is the one who says that the mind is capable of reversing the process of entropy, and that's ridiculous. I work with what is real, you understand; I don't work with dreams. It's easy to use what you know to stuff other people's minds full of nonsense.'

His attitude upset me, and increased my doubts: one should not confuse mental and mechanical disorder. He said, 'What you're saying has no basis in reality whatsoever. You can't prove a thing. You can't take a thermodynamic fact, however simple, and deduce behavioural reactions from it. That's nonsense. You can make any word mean anything you like. You have a poetic attitude towards facts – there's nothing scientific about that.'

My arguments lacked precision and I couldn't put them into an equation. I could register the production and reproduction of certain isolated events, but I couldn't predict their appearance, much less their recurrence . . . Listening to him, I realised that I had simply been rambling.

I showed him some of my favourite quotations, some of the ones I had pinned above my desk, which gave me courage, which set me dreaming:

The unification by the theory of relativity of the notions of time and space introduced a harmony which did not exist before. (P. Langevin, *La Relativité*)

In relative physics, one must no longer consider space and time separately, or give a universal character to time; in a manner it is necessary to merge space and time in a four-dimensional continuum, the space-time of Einstein or the universe of Minkowski, where every observer carves out in his own way his space and time. (L. de Broglie, *Physics and Microphysics*)

He read these words as if I were punishing him for misbehaving. Then he grumbled, 'Where did you get this?'

'Your office.'

'What! I never realised that you ferreted amongst my things like that . . . So?'

'I would like you to tell me about *your* way of dividing up space and time. I'd like you to tell me about *your* thermo-dynamics. I'd like you to admit that the laws are what each person makes of them. That what you use in physics may also be useful to me in psychology. That I, too, relatively, can work with energy, work, disorder, order . . . You do exactly the same thing as I do, except that with you it's physics, so it's serious, and with me it's psychology, so it's nonsense . . .'

'If you like. Go ahead and work, my dear, think. There's no point trying to stop people saying and doing stupid things! Listen, Luce, I'm not a psychologist, I'm not an intellectual, I'm a scientist and I don't give a damn about individuals. You know that. You've reproached me often enough for not distinguishing between one woman and another. I don't like philosophers – they talk and they say nothing.'

'All the great philosophers have also been scientists.'

'Scientists gone wrong . . . In my youth I thought a lot about a phrase of Aristotle's: "Probable impossibilities are to be preferred to improbable possibilities." Claptrap . . . Absolute claptrap!'

'And yet – '

'Claptrap, I tell you! Nothing but claptrap!'

I went back to see him. We had never talked about me so much before. I wanted to believe in what I had believed in. I told him about my research on hormones. I considered hormones to be like any other junction point in a system. They improved performance while increasing instances of overheating, and thus losses of energy, entropy. The action of neuro-hormones on the pituitary gland, for example, was well known, so how could anyone resist the temptation to assert that the workings of the human machine are also affected by these substances? How could anyone not take them into account? How could anyone not accept that 'personalities' owe some of their traits to these substances? How could anyone not admit that the mind is also matter, like temperature, which can be measured and yet which is not a thing?

He listened to me more closely because it wasn't exactly his field. He nodded his head as if to say: 'It's possible, it's possible. I don't know anything about it. That's not my area.'

I thought I had convinced him. I pushed my arguments, I justified my procedure, and whenever I stopped to let him give me his opinion, each time he said, 'And I thought you were interested in my work because you were interested in me . . . Was it really the other way round?' He looked at me like someone dredging his memory for a dream. 'But you loved me. You loved me all those years . . .'

'Yes, I loved you . . . I owe you a lot . . . But as you know perfectly well, I've always had a job, a daughter . . . my own life. You were never interested.'

He didn't want to talk any longer. He didn't want to hear me any longer. He took my hand and placed it on his penis; he wanted me to stroke it. It was very sad. I no longer had any desire for the penis which I had used so often, with which I had given myself so much pleasure. The saddest thing was that I knew his penis didn't matter to him, either. It was just an apparatus that women admired, a simple machine that had always worked, that had always been like that – unmysterious, uninteresting. He wanted to be loved for something other than that, the penis swelling under the flannel of his trousers, warm, silky, docile, infinitely adorable – and useless. It was all we had left.

I don't believe I have ever been in such a distressing situation as we were in then. We were in such a private, intimate position: he stretched out on his bed, me sitting on the edge of the bed next to him, my hand on his penis, his hand holding mine there, in the yellow light of the bedside lamp. In that brief moment we came to a very accurate assessment of the emptiness of our relationship . . . It was absolute zero, death, where the temperature is the same everywhere.

I don't know where his mind went off to – I no longer wish to try and guess how other people's minds escape – but I know that mine wandered off on such a vertiginous, harrowing journey that the only way to quell the fear that filled me then would be death. If only the days would stop; if only today would not happen again; if only my little fire would go out.

I told him that I was overcome with despair. He put my

despair through his personal still and concluded that he was the one driving me to despair.

I tried to talk about Laure and what I'd gone through with her, about the brutal shock that heroin had given me. He then thought that I was speaking as a mother, that Laure's mum had been hurt. He soothed me with clumsy words, stock phrases that childless people use when speaking to those who have children. He was astonished that I, who was 'so intelligent', had let Laure surprise me. I told him it was nothing, it was all over, it was all in the past. I was going to rest and everything would fall back into place; order would be restored. He even seemed relieved. He thought he finally understood why I had resigned. It wasn't serious; perhaps I would come back, perhaps I would love him again. He had found those three years without me very long . . .

I haven't seen him since, and it's been a long time now.

PART THREE

I'm extending my trip. I'm nowhere, stuck there.

What's the point in going back to Paris? It's summer; I won't find any work. The editorial departments of newspapers and publishing houses are aestivating. For two months the only people to be found there are a few unhappy souls waiting for their holidays to start, or other unhappy souls recovering from their holidays. There's no work to be had. When you're unhappy, Paris in summer is enough to make you want to shoot yourself.

I like my neighbourhood – the bistro on the corner where I gulp my coffee in the morning, because I'm late, and the big café on the main boulevard that flashes all its golden lights at night to attract stragglers to the bar or cigarette counter . . . I like the baker and her daughter, who's quite a flirt; her mother's going to have her hands full. She's only thirteen, but she's already got a nice wiggle. Where do girls learn that? When I was thirteen . . . Forget it. I like the butcher a lot, too. He's a real rugby fan; he never misses a match. He's in a club that follows the French national team wherever it plays during the Five Nations Tournament. When the match is abroad, he leaves Friday night and comes back Sunday. I once saw him leave his shop wearing a red, white and blue muffler and a tweed cap: he looked rather formidable. His wife and three kids followed him, waving paper tricolours, running to keep him in sight. They went with him to the Gare du Nord . . . We talk while he cuts my steaks. To him, there's France on one side, and Ireland, Scotland, Wales and England on the other. The rest of the world consists mainly of New Zealand and Australia, and that's about it. No one else plays rugger.

The shops are closed now; it's summer.

I'm like the butcher – except my world isn't rugby, it's Elsa.

I called home with my remote control to see if there were any messages on my answering machine. She telephoned me the ninth of August, just leaving her name, the date and the time of her call. Methodical, always methodical! Prepared! I hate Elsa when she's methodical! I hate her. She's my worst enemy. I love Elsa when she's mad.

I'm not going back to Paris until I've made a choice: either I clear off, drop everything, and too bad for the book – I'll never see her again – or I go straight over to her place and say, 'Elsa, I love you. I want to live with you.'

Just like that. It's crazy; that's the crazy choice.

I arrive at her place. She opens the door, I go in, and there in the hall, I say, 'Elsa, I love you.' She's wearing a plain summer dress, white linen, perhaps. She's barefoot. She often goes barefoot. I don't know how many times I've seen her in her tartan skirt and her black shetland twin set, all very chic, with no shoes. Oh, I love her. There's no use fighting it.

I go in. She's barefoot. She's wearing her old jeans and a T-shirt. I say, 'Elsa, I love you.' What does she do? There are a number of possibilities:

1. Quick as a flash, she answers, 'Go on, you're young enough to be my son.'

Elsa's done it all; she's seen it all. She's capable of anything, but convention matters to her. I wouldn't be surprised if she said that, even though it isn't quite true that I'm young enough to be her son. I've never felt the age difference between us, but I'm sure that it exists for her, carefully filed away in her personal set of rules and regulations.

2. She looks at me with her flecked, light brown eyes, verging on yellow, almost the colour of her hair, and says nothing. But in those eyes I've seen her innocence, that capacity of hers to take everything seriously, to be interested in everything. It takes a few seconds for her to get over her surprise and analyse the question. A few seconds for me to turn from Romeo into Don Quixote. She asks me into the sitting room. I sit down in 'my' armchair, she on 'her' cushion, and I start babbling. I ruin everything. She makes me do an about-face; she demonstrates with a plus b that

what I think is love isn't really love at all, that I've made a transference. And we return to the set of rules and regulations of the first answer, this time via scientific convention. I can't find a way around it. Bye-bye love, bye-bye happiness!

3. I go in. She's wearing her grey suit with her nice moccasins, and she has that look she puts on for important occasions, her Pythian gaze. Once again, she's in the midst of remaking the world from top to bottom. Her face, her movements, her body all say that she is trying to understand the meaning of life and death. She's so intelligent, so lucid, so passionate, so tragic that I would rather drop dead than confess my pathetic love.

4. I go in; I say, 'Elsa, I love you.' She is facing me, tall and erect like the Statue of Liberty at the entrance to New York harbour. She whips my head around with a good slap . . . No, she wouldn't do that, she has too much respect for people's feelings.

5. My own Elsa opens the door. I don't have to say a word. She has understood everything. She knows her place is in my arms, and my place is in her arms. It's all very simple. There are just the two of us, sweetly, tenderly . . . Sure thing. Not a hope in hell. I don't have a chance in a million of it happening like that.

The best thing to do is to take a break in the country with my parents. Move back into my good old bedroom, take my manuscript out of my travelling bag – I haven't even looked at it in ten days – and work, get this out of my head. I've got myself into an unbelievable mess. Up until now Writing has solved all my problems, so I don't see why she shouldn't solve this one. Come, my lovely, put on your letter-lace dress and let the castanets of my typewriter resound. That's the most beautiful music there is. You and I have been through worse.

I've been here two weeks now, and Writing is sulking on me; she's jealous. Indoors, my mother's jam smells too good and outdoors, my father's garden is too pretty. Life here is too regular, too happy, too straight. Everything is too easy, too gentle, too tender – because it's happening without her.

Because it's goodness, gentleness, ease, tenderness, that she isn't enjoying. Any pleasure without Elsa is stolen pleasure. My pleasure belongs to her, my happiness belongs to her. I can't stay here any longer. I'm going back.

Back to the suburbs, the old city gates, my neighbourhood, my street, my building, my tape recorder, her voice. Back to her.

I'm not getting anywhere. It's rush hour. My carburettor is acting up. I keep stalling. There are traffic jams at Denfert-Rochereau. And yet the holidays aren't over yet. What are all these people doing in Paris?

The smell. The smell of the Métro and of car exhaust. The smell of my city. The smell of my adult life. The smell of the man that I have become here, in the maze of streets, with the Eiffel Tower as the focal point between two Haussmann buildings. My memory serves as Paris's memory. The City of Lights has no memory. She doesn't care whether she is built up or falls down; she puts up no resistance. My life and death are of no consequence to her. She is my chimera or my cloaca, my heaven or my cemetery, whichever I choose; she is whatever I want, depending on the day. Today, because I'm afraid, she is making a display of the things I invented to conquer my fears, and since my fears persist, she frightens me, too. I stand up to her; I tell her that she's suffocating me, poisoning me. I haven't even reached Fontainebleau when I begin to search the sky for her pollution. She doesn't pollute any more than she remembers. She is the womb I have chosen to be born in. I have made this mother for myself with my jobs, bistros, loves, wanderings, bridges, palaces, arcs of triumph and dream villas. She has sewers, rubbish tips, city dumps, but nowhere to dispose of my cowardice and mediocrity. They remain stuck to her walls along with shreds of posters, souvenirs of old shows, stars of frustration, constellations of my shit.

I get the creeps whenever I enter your guts, my capital reeking of cold fag ends and hot tar, my whore bedizened with neon lights and Wallace fountains. I'm scared to death. Please, be nice, let Elsa be there, at home, quiet, happy to see me. Be kind, I beg of you. I'm your prodigal son; look,

I'm home. I'll go light a candle at Montmartre if you like, or at the Folies Bergère if you'd rather. I can become a tramp or a tourist to please you, or a bus driver, or a sidewalk oyster vendor in Montparnasse. Please don't be nasty, because misery here is worse than misery anywhere else. But you don't really give a damn about anything I'm saying; you're deaf; you're nothing but a city.

In any case, not all the Parisians have come back, because I've found a parking place on my own street right near where I live. It's a good sign; perhaps the capital did hear my prayer, after all.

My letter-box is stuffed with flyers, bills and all the bumf that turns up in a letter-box the minute you turn your back. And, and, and – two letters from Elsa. Two letters from Elsa! I'd recognise her handwriting anywhere; I spent enough time deciphering it in the passages about Professor Greffier. Hmm, I'd forgotten about him. What can I do? I'm only a poor ghost writer, a writer of pulp thrillers. What can I do up against a guy like that? I'm just no match. In the lift I check the postmarks. They were posted near her place. But what's the matter with me? My heart is beating wildly. I can't find my keys; I'm getting myself into a state. I drop the post on the floor in the corridor; I spend an age picking it up. I'm off to a good start, off to a flying start.

It's stuffy in here. It never even occurred to me to leave a window open. I don't know where my mind has been lately. I remember Elsa saying, 'I'm so absent-minded these days. You have no idea how absent-minded I've become.' That was just before she went off the deep end . . .

In any case, before opening her letters I'm going to make some coffee and get settled in. Because Elsa can write things that bowl me right over. I'd better prepare myself.

A letter posted on the twelfth, three days after she left her message on my answering machine: 'It's Elsa, five in the afternoon, August the ninth . . .' Elsa. Elsa! It hadn't occurred to me before. 'It's Elsa, five in the afternoon, August the ninth.' She only calls herself Elsa to herself and to me. I should have thought about it; it must mean something. I'll think about it later.

I mustn't drink too much coffee. My heart is pounding so hard it feels as though it's about to break through my ribs and start jumping about the sitting room, like a grasshopper, bop, bop, bop, all the way to the door: Bye, everyone.

OK, let's not get carried away. I'm not writing a thriller.

Letter number one:

Hello, hello there!

You know what – I've forgotten your first name. I've just realised, as I sat down to write this letter, that I've never called you anything but 'you'. Not wanting to hurt your feelings, I tried to look it up in Dr Bourget's book, but you aren't even mentioned . . . I looked in the street directory and found the initial P. Pierre? Patrick? Philippe? Paul? I even went through the telephone directory. It can't be Pedro, or Philibert, or Philémon, or Pancrace, or Pantaléon – I would have remembered that.

So hello there, you. I hope my lapse of memory doesn't shock you.

I wanted to write because I miss you and I can't wait to see you again. I've thought of all kinds of things. We'll go all the way this time.

Enjoy your holiday.

Your affectionate friend,

Elsa

It's a nice letter, not sad. Yes, that's it, nice, that's all. Nothing to get excited about.

What else did I expect? What more did I want her to write? And why would she have written anything more? In honour of what?

Letter number two, a thick one:

Hello!

I'm leaving tonight with Laure for Aix. We're going to spend a few days with my parents. Are you having your post forwarded?

Will you be back in Paris before I am? I'll be back on 3 September.

In case you're still interested in doing the book (I didn't know how to interpret your sudden departure. Are you simply abandoning the whole thing?), here is an outline of the ideas I would like to develop to bring it to a close:

– Heroin is a love story. You get into it because it gives the illusion of being absolute (ecstasy, rush) and you escape from it through passion (orgasm). The absolute and passion, the two main avenues of love.

– When they start on drugs, users contract an illness – addiction, dependency – and it's only through another addiction, another dependency, that they ever get out.

– Addiction to hard drugs is a terminal illness. To cure a drug addict you'd have to get him off one passion and hooked on another. But that's the ideal. The first phase of the operation is easy with the right pharmacopœia, but the second phase is scientifically impossible. Complete knowledge of the physiology and psychology of a drug user (knowing why and how she or he achieves ecstasy) cannot be used to help her or him achieve another ecstasy or orgasm. Unfortunately, and also fortunately, that is a mystery science is powerless to solve. It is questionable whether a cure can be found: what orgasm can equal ecstasy? The only one who can answer that is the person concerned, and then only after experiencing the right orgasm, that is, after being cured.

– Knowledge corrupts instinct.

– Orgasm, in its fullness, has nothing to do with sex.

– 1 and 2. One and two. Only two can make knowledge work. Knowledge has no access to one. Drug addicts and mystics succeed in becoming one. One is nothing: it is inhuman, incomprehensible, beyond the human condition.

All this has to be put in context and I don't know how to do it. I need you, because you know how to write fiction.

Since you've been away, I've been going over these ideas in my mind, looking for anecdotes, images. I thought of Mademoiselle Véla, my catechism teacher.

She was bandy-legged. She walked backwards. I can't imagine Mademoiselle Véla walking any other way. She led us, backwards, from our class-room to the catechism room or the chapel. On important occasions, when we had to go to the parish church, she would face us as she walked along the pavement. She would cross the streets backwards, confronting – so to speak – the traffic, cars and trams coming and going, like that, in reverse, reading the danger signs in our eyes. She really had a blind faith in us. What was most important to her – the most important thing in her life – was that on the way to His sanctuary we should look like little girls in whom Christ dwelt, and she couldn't have borne seeing us publicly holding her beloved up to ridicule. It's true that her imposing bearing and our great responsibility subdued us. There was absolutely no question of us falling out of order or playing her up.

Her greying hair was braided and pulled back into a bun at the nape of her neck, giving her a smooth, shiny skull, a sort of cap that thrust the thick features of her nose, mouth and chin forward, drawing more attention to her ugliness. But she had gentle eyes and wonderful utterances came out of her mouth: the first love stories I ever heard. Mary Magdalene wiping Christ's feet with her long red hair (why red?), the face of the beloved imprinted on Veronica's cloth . . . The loaves and the fishes that multiplied, the dead who were resurrected, the deep water that became a raft – all for love of Him, all to glorify the love He bore us! I, too, wanted to love the peaceful bearded man who had fallen asleep in the shroud. I wanted to believe.

At morning mass – 'in silence and contemplation,' said Mademoiselle Véla – I would kneel in contemplation, silent but impatient. I kept hoping that the miracle would happen, that He and I would love each other. The sun rose behind the stained glass windows of the chancel and I could see the crucifix on the altar, against the light, sublimely incandescent. The glow of the light, the shining gold, was tangible proof that God existed. I lowered my head and repeated: 'Dear God, I love you. Jesus, I love you.' I believed that if I said this over and over the love would become a reality. But it never did; it remained theoretical. I wasn't in love. In Mademoiselle Véla's eyes, however, I could see that this love was possible. I saw the flood of love imbuing her and fulfilling her.

For a long time I laboured under the impression that my inability to love God was a moral flaw. Later, when I loved Jacques, I sometimes felt guilty about not loving God as I loved that man. I was certain that what I felt for Jacques was comparable to what Mademoiselle Véla felt for Christ: an exaltation, a warm openness, a desire for the other, for all of the other, a contemplation of the other, of all of the other, from his head to his feet, along with his desires, all his desires, including the desire for sacrifice. Except that Christ didn't exist, while Jacques had a body; I could see it, touch it, hear it, smell it . . .

And he had a sex organ through which breathtaking desires were expressed . . .

Despite all the love I felt for Jacques, I envied Mademoiselle Véla.

After Jacques died, there was something mystical about the bond that tied me to him. Widowhood conferred upon me a serenity I didn't really have. I loved someone who was elsewhere, not of this world, in a completely satisfying way. I was both of the here and now and of the hereafter, of the Great Beyond. In the Great Beyond there was the idea of Jacques. His spirit – and his living body, too. I never compared myself to Saint Teresa of Avila, Saint John of the Cross, or the Québécoise Marie de l'Incarnation – all those people who levitate, cry tears of blood, and crawl on the ceiling as easily as I go to market. I never thought of ecstasy . . . But why – through what hypocritical inhibition, what ridiculous devoutness? – did I never make the connection between ecstasy and orgasm? Between orgasm and the soul?

My strange relationship with Professor Greffier did not destroy what widowhood had given me. That penis at my disposal, as beautiful as the man himself was ugly, as attentive as the man was indifferent, as docile as the man was possessive. That male organ, as independent as if it did not belong to the man at all, as if it were the magnificat of sex, as if it were sexuality incarnate, as if it were abstract despite its firmness . . .

I've been thinking about what I said into the tape recorder a few weeks ago about the heart and sex: intimacy and privacy, continuity and discontinuity, and their connection, which would be the path to the soul. I was talking as I'm writing today, letting words flow freely. And yet these words have a life of their own and I realise that I transcended my private life, my sex life. I acted as if sex did not exist. I attained ecstasy, an altered state of consciousness, through knowledge. What did I think about while I was making love with Professor Greffier's penis, by myself? Not about him anyway. Orgasm is experienced in solitude.

Why be afraid to establish a connection between orgasm and ecstasy? I approach words with an innocence that borders on stupidity. They can have the same effect on me as a puppet show or a magician has on children. They dazzle me, sometimes make me blindingly dizzy . . . Orgasm, ecstasy. Why should one be considered sacred but not the other? The two lead to the same result: a swoon, rapture, absolute escape from the material world, absolute solitude, total confusion between what is and is not, weightlessness, floating . . . Finally realising the dream of Icarus . . . Why is sex so impure? Why has it been perverted to such a degree? Why has the word love been given this perverse ambiguity? Why be guilty of loving with one's body or of not loving with one's spirit? Why is sex the prime locus of impurity? Hard-core heroin addicts, real junkies, have practically no sex life. The syringe transcends sex. Why do some human beings end up having to get high to be pure? Pure is a word I heard a lot when I was living in the midst of drug addicts. Pure and junk! 'It's good stuff, it's pure.' And dealers have a thousand and one ways of corrupting its purity, to the point where when it's too pure, it kills those who have only ever used it cut . . .

I lived only in the absolute, like Laure. All passions tend toward the absolute, and are addictive. But I didn't realise that. I had erroneous, restrictive notions of passion and the absolute.

I'm well: I've found equilibrium . . . Let's say I feel that I'm the centre of my universe – except I don't understand my universe. But I do know where I am, at least. That's real progress. By making me aware of the narrowness – and especially the pretentiousness – of my knowledge, heroin increased my doubts and uncertainties, and deprived me of desire. I was afraid of my curiosity, and avoided it. Today, thanks to you, I am no longer avoiding it. Did you know that you saved my life?

I hope that you aren't too angry, and that you'll be there when I get back. I miss you.

Your friend,

Elsa

The only thing I get out of the letter is that she isn't there. What the hell am I going to do for five days? I'm going to go stark raving mad.

One and two. Mademoiselle Véla . . . The woman can't even sit still for five minutes! How can I think about that when I've got only one thing on my mind: I love her.

Mademoiselle Véla is a great character. I can easily imagine her leading a double life. Catechism teacher by day, whore, like Mary Magdalene, by night. She would offer herself up to men as if she were a host. The story would have an unhappy ending. They'd find her body in the early morning hours, on the steps of a church. What tripe. I can't suggest that to Elsa. Although you never know with her.

I can't sleep. Time seems to have stopped. I keep looking at my watch. It doesn't move. What is she doing in Aix? She's with Laure. I've only seen them together once, but that's enough for me to imagine what goes on between them: chatter, laughter, secrets. Laure probably talks about her boyfriend. Does Elsa talk about the book? Does she talk about me? Do I exist for her? Am I anything but a ghost writer?

I could call her, ask directory enquiries for the number of the shop in Aix. But I don't know her parents' last name. She doesn't go by their name, she goes by her husband's.

And then, even if I called, what would I say? 'Hello. I'm in Paris les Bains de Pieds. How are you? Everything all right?' But ringing her up wouldn't work unless I had something intelligent to say about the book, and I don't have anything like that to offer. I can't think any more; I no longer have anything going on in my head.

All that's in my head is her voice, her hair, her hands, her legs – legs never age. Her eyes, especially her eyes. She often makes me think of a photograph. Who's it by again? Riboud, I think, but I'm not sure any more. A picture of the face of a deaf child hearing his voice for the first time. He's wearing headphones, or some sort of device, but you see only his eyes, wide open, astonished, enchanted. He's hearing inside himself . . . Elsa often has that look. And I just melt when I see that. I feel like a knight: Don't be afraid, Elsa, I'm here. I, Lancelot of the Whodunnit. I've got my helmet and my coat of mail, my broadsword and my steed. Up you get, into the saddle and off we go. Hold on tight – goodbye theremodynamics and all that jazz. Don't be afraid, we're off to paradise, Elsa, my dear . . .

Why do I want to protect her? She's ten times stronger than I am.

She's strong, but she's also as fragile as she is strong.

And then there's that attentive, credulous look of hers, that good-schoolgirl look. She listens, she learns, she's self-confident; she's going to put everything away in her little school-bag and tomorrow she'll know it all by heart and she'll understand everything. You can make Elsa believe anything. All she wants is to believe, learn, open up, know.

But there is also her wild look, her look of solitude. She doesn't want to know anything more, she doesn't want to receive any more and she doesn't want to give any more. If not for that look, I would have told her a long time ago that I loved her. But she is formidable when she is hurt, when she withdraws within herself. She's inaccessible.

I'm quite an ordinary bloke, quite average. I'm not short or tall, fat or thin, handsome or ugly; I don't even have a moustache, or wear glasses, either. And until I met Elsa, I led a life that matched my appearance, an easy life, a life that was easy to appreciate. Only my books aren't appreciated; they aren't appreciated at all. I must be unequal to my imagination; I render it poorly.

This morning one of the papers phoned me. They wanted

to send me off to investigate some mystery near Belfort. I turned them down. A year ago I would have jumped for joy. Not only would have I done anything to work for that paper, but that type of assignment would have really excited me. I told them I wasn't available. I can't leave Paris; I want to be here when Elsa gets back.

Last night, to get my mind onto other things, I rang up an old girl-friend. We've known each other a long time and like each other a lot. There's no nonsense between us, and there never has been. She was tickled to hear from me. 'Paris is deserted. Everyone's away.' We met in a bistro. She was dressed to the nines, a nice intelligent girl with big boobs. We spent the evening together and I took her home with me. But there was nothing doing. Nothing. She went to all kinds of trouble. Zero. Nothing.

'What's the matter? Are you OK? I've never seen you like this before.'

'Forget it. Let's talk about something else. I'm sorry.'

'Is it my dress? Did I say something to turn you off?'

'Please, I'm humiliated enough already. But it's nothing to do with you, not at all. You've been really great. I had a nice evening. It's me. I'm not myself right now.'

All I could think about was getting rid of her. I took her home, excusing myself over and over again.

I'm impotent, Elsa.

Two more days.

Ever since what happened with my girl-friend, things have been going from bad to worse. I turned down the newspaper assignment, and I've been hanging about at home, doing nothing. I didn't even watch an old film that was on the TV, which I normally like to do. I just changed the channel.

I'm in withdrawal; it's quite obvious. There's no point trying to hide it any longer, or trying to complicate the issue. I'm in withdrawal. I need Elsa, I need her badly. I never would have believed that something like this could happen to me and yet it has.

Two more nights and one day to get through. It's unbearable.

I rummage through my medicine chest. There must be

an old packet of sleeping tablets from years ago in there somewhere. I take two tablets and conk out right away. I have just enough time to feel sleep overcoming me and it feels good to be released from Elsa.

The phone is ringing. Good God, the phone is ringing! It can go on ringing for all I care! The phone is ringing. All you have to do is lift your hand – it's right there on the floor by the bed. What if it's Elsa? What time is it? What day is it?

'Hello!'

'Hello, is that you? Hello?'

'Hello, hello. Who is it?'

'It's Elsa.'

My head is like an overripe watermelon, bright red with black seeds, full of black seeds.

'Did I wake you up? Sorry.'

'No, I wasn't asleep, I was just . . . making some coffee.'

'I'm sorry to disturb you.'

'Not at all, not at all. You're not disturbing me. Are you in Paris? Is it the third?'

'No, I'm in Aix. I'm coming back tomorrow. I'm looking forward to going home. Did you get my letters?'

'Yes, I did.'

'What did you think?'

'What did I think of what?'

'Of what I wrote, Mademoiselle Véla, all that?'

'It's great, it's good material.'

'I think we're approaching it the right way. We're going to finish the book . . . I thought that we could get together, we could have dinner together. How about it?'

'That's a great idea. When?'

'Tomorrow. I'm arriving some time in the afternoon. How about tomorrow evening?'

'What time do you want me to come over?'

'No, don't come to my place. Let's go somewhere else. We have to celebrate the end of our project. And we've never met anywhere else before.'

'OK. Where?'

'I don't know. I rarely dine out. Can you think of a place?'

'Let's see . . . We could go to the Louis XIV, at Place des Victoires.'

'If it's not too fancy. You don't have to dress up, I hope?'

'No, it's a simple little place, a bistro. The food is good.'

'Fine. Tomorrow, then, at about half past eight or nine?'

'Half past eight.'

'Wonderful. I'm really looking forward to seeing you again. You're going to be surprised – I've got everything worked out in my head.'

'Good, good.'

'See you tomorrow, then.'

'Yes, see you tomorrow.'

It was over; Elsa was gone. Lost in the telecommunications network. Had she ever had such an idiotic conversation? Had she ever talked to a guy as idiotic as I am? She's all excited, happy to be coming home, and she invites me out to dinner . . . and all I can say is yes, no, yes, no. What had I thought of her letters? Not much: 'Great, great . . .' It's just lucky that I suggested the Louis XIV; I could quite as easily have suggested the local café, where they serve dried-up cold meat and rancid quiche. But what if the Louis XIV is closed on September third?

It wasn't closed. I booked a table upstairs by a window, from where you can see the square all lit up, the statue of the Sun King on his horse in the middle, and a pretty building on the other side.

At twenty past eight I was there, but she wasn't. As usual, I'm always early. What shall I do? Should I sit at the table? Go outside? I go out. I pace up and down outside the restaurant. It's a warm evening, still summer. The night sky of Paris is pink above the rooftops. Pink and mauve. Pink and mauve and deep blue.

A car door slams. Why should I look in the direction of the slammed door? Because Elsa slammed it. And yet I've never seen her slam a car door, never seen her car, never seen Elsa outside. I've never seen Elsa moving freely about the city.

My darling approaches. She hasn't seen me; she's looking at her reflection in a window along the way, arranging a wisp of hair. There isn't another woman more beautiful than she is. She's even more beautiful than I remembered. She's extraordinary. She's love in motion. She's the present and the future striding boldly along.

I shouldn't have stayed outside. Now I'm standing here looking helpless. Whatever became of Lancelot of the Whodunnit? Off fighting some stupid war, probably. That fool is never around when he's needed . . . She sees me and smiles. She's tanned. How can she be tanned? She looks younger. Where did she and Laure run off to? They know how to enjoy themselves, those two. They're thick as thieves.

Hello. Hello. Fortunately women walk ahead of men on occasions like this. That way she can't see my face, and I have some time to compose myself. She's wearing a plain pink linen dress and sandals, showing her great legs.

She likes it. She likes everything: the restaurant, the table, the view, the flowers on the table. So much the better; at least I've done something right.

She's in a good mood, funny, talkative . . . She's met someone, I'm sure she's met someone, while yours truly . . . She talks about the book; she says that the book has set her free; that it's all thanks to me . . . I listen to her, and I should be pleased. But I'm not listening to her, I'm thinking about the guy she's met.

'Did you spend time at the beach?'

She gives me her good-schoolgirl look, trying to understand.

'What beach?'

'You're so tanned.'

'That's Aix for you. We spent all our time in the garden. There's a large plane tree and a small lawn, just big enough for Laure and me. We spent our days on the grass talking, the two of us in the sun and my parents in the shade of the tree.'

'In the centre of town.'

'Yes, right in the centre of town, in the midst of the tourist sites of old Aix. Fortunately our street has been turned into a pedestrian street. On the garden side you'd think you were in the country.'

'And how's the shop doing?'

'My parents have hired an assistant and a cashier. My mother is tired, and so is my father. He supervises . . . I tan very fast and Laure even faster. It was great – we ate all our meals in the garden. We only left the house a couple of times for a pastis at an outdoor café in the evening, when it was cool . . .'

Laure this, Laure that, Laure does fabulous things, Laure wants to have a baby . . . I'm shrivelling up on my chair, dumbfounded by my stupidity. In my view, when a woman is happy and beautiful there's got to be a guy in the picture. But Elsa doesn't have a guy. She's beautiful and happy because Laure is doing well and because she's thinking about the book.

She asks me politely about my holidays. I say they were terrific, couldn't have been better . . . If she only knew.

She moves on to Mademoiselle Véla. I feel so hopeless, so overwhelmed by events, so unequal to the situation, that suddenly, risking all, I plunge in: I talk about the murder of Mademoiselle Véla, her body found at dawn on the square in front of St Ambroise's Church. Elsa stares at me with that mute-child look, which always shakes me. She can't believe what she's hearing. She simply asks:

'Where's St Ambroise's Church?'

'I have no idea. There must be a St Ambroise's Church somewhere in Christendom.'

'At night she's a prostitute?'

'She gives herself up to be consumed, like Christ. It's her way of emulating Jesus. A living host . . . I consider that the consumption of prostitutes is similar to the cannibalism of communion.'

'And does she have orgasms?'

'No, ecstasies. Each time she is penetrated. That's why she comes to a bad end.'

'Why?'

'Because prostitutes don't generally have orgasms. They provide services, that's all . . . But one of her customers realises that she is climaxing and that the climax is abnormal. He realises that he's been misled about the merchandise, that this woman puts something sacred into what he sees as only the profane, only the lowest type of sexuality. He's shocked.

Because the man is a religious nut-case, a Dostoyevskian character. One day he suggests that he shouldn't pay her and she refuses.'

'Why?'

'Because it's the money that humiliates her the most, that's the hardest part for her, that makes her night-time ecstasies so important to her.'

'Does the customer understand that?'

'No, he thinks she's venal, a walking sacrilege.'

'But both of them are addicted . . .'

'Yes, addicted to God.'

'We can't develop that in the book; it would be another book, but it's interesting . . .'

She leans over her *brochet beurre blanc* and stares down at it, mechanically pushing a bit of fish with her fork. I have the feeling she's making a tremendous effort not to laugh in my face. She thinks I'm a fool . . . Why did I have to go and tell her the story of Mademoiselle Véla as a prostitute? What came over me? I've put my foot right in it, ruined everything. She's upset. I put myself in her place. She's got a book on drugs, on the powerlessness of science and knowledge to solve the drug problem. A book on love, too . . . And I dish her up a stupid story about a prostitute and a fanatic. With a murder in it, of course. Blood everywhere . . . It's not even a grade B story, it's grade W. I wish the earth would open up and swallow me. I'd like to disappear, erase what I said, and start the film over from when we met downstairs on the street. We would have fallen into each other's arms like lovers; we wouldn't even have gone to the restaurant; we would have strolled along the Seine without speaking – without exchanging a word. Me and my crime stories . . . How do I invent stories like that when I lead such a dull existence? The only drama in my life is having met Elsa. She says that drugs reveal a lot. To me, *she* reveals a lot. I'm just a dead loss, nothing but a dead loss.

I've been reducing my rare – 'Very rare, if possible' – chateaubriand to ribbons for a while now. No subtlety, no point being subtle, old chap . . .

I feel like I'll never dare look up again. And yet I must.

She must still be contemplating her fish bones . . . She

could at least say something, though. What's the point of leaving me staring at my food. All right, so I'm a fool. We're all agreed on that score. She can see that we agree, that I'm fully aware of it . . . My throat and eyes are stinging. I want to go home and have a good sob . . . I've thought too much about this dinner. It was going to be so beautiful; I invented too much of Elsa.

She's moved. I lift my head. She looks at me. She has a look in her eye I've never seen before. I think – but it's crazy – that she must look at Laure like that when they're by themselves. She doesn't lower her eyes, she keeps staring at me. She opens the door. I enter into her penumbra. I knew it would be like that inside: ferns, moss, velvet. A hearth for Lancelot, tall and deep, with a crackling fire. Books, lots of big books. Picture books, too. Water: running water and still water. And far off in the distance – sunlight. A beach with seagulls, waves and sailing boats. It smells of the sea; you can hear the surf.

She motions with her hand. It's over. Closed. Her look has changed. I'm sitting. She's facing me. She's speaking: 'I don't think I've told you how grateful I am. I'll never forget your visits, your gifts, everything you did for me when I couldn't speak any more. You know, all those things you brought me. I didn't touch them. One day I put them all in the kitchen. All that stuff was meant for me; it represented a relationship between someone and me . . . between you and me . . . I sat down before it; I examined it all; I tried to understand who I was, who the woman to whom you gave those gifts was. You got to know the real me and each object suited me. But what disorder they made all together! It was mad . . . I've always tried to control my disorder . . . No, not always . . . Ever since I went to claim Jacques's body at Port Vendres with Laure, ever since I found myself alone with her, I've considered my disorder to be our worst enemy and have done everything I could to protect her from it . . . I was in the kitchen, looking at this pile of stuff, and I was confronting twenty years of my order, my rules, my discipline, choices I had made and which I had lived by very strictly . . . I thought I was lost, I thought I would never find myself again . . . My energy drained out of me, and I didn't leave my bedroom any more. That's when you put the tape recorder on my bedside table . . . The idea of talking to the pile in the kitchen, of talking to myself, came to me. That heap was me, my disorder, what was best in me. I said that I was useless, that I didn't understand Laure, that I didn't understand anything – I, who claimed to understand other people . . . For twenty years all I had done was protect myself from love . . . In the end, love, pure and simple, is much more difficult to live with than passion, the absolute . . . The absolute is a refuge . . . Laure got out of it, and I had to get out of it too, or I would have died . . . I talked, talked, talked of the fortress in which I had taken shelter, about thermodynamics, about Professor Greffier, about my career . . . You know all that now. I owe you my life. Without you I would have let myself die. Today I'm fine. I can't get over it. I don't think I've ever been so happy to be alive.'

'Because you're no longer in withdrawal.'

She finds that amusing, I can see it in her eyes. Once again, but scarcely, for only a brief second, she gives me her affectionate look.

'You're funny. I really like the way you handle problems. It surprises me and appeals to me. It's so simple . . . I'm no longer in withdrawal from what?'

'Elsa the scientist. You don't need her any more.'

'I don't know . . . While we were in Aix, I talked to Laure. She didn't know I'd stopped working. I wound up telling her because my parents are in a dilemma. They're too old and they can't keep up any more. Either they have to get someone to manage the shop or sell the business. It's a big problem. They have virtually no choice but to move, because the shop without the upstairs flat wouldn't fetch enough . . . So we were talking about all that and I said to Laure, "We could take over the shop. You could be the saleswoman and I could be the cashier." I was joking, of course, but only partly. Laure realised that my suggestion was half-serious. You should have heard her laugh . . . She couldn't stop – I thought she was going to choke. She was shrieking with joy, "No, no, no, you'd be the saleswoman! It would do you good to fondle sexy underpants, half-cup bras, and lace slips with little cross-stitch roses! And I'd be on the till. It would be perfect! It would teach me to count: once I get past two plus two equals four, I'm hopeless with numbers . . ." We laughed like mad imagining it all . . . No, I don't want to break with Elsa the scientist, I just don't want her to come first any more . . . But you're right, I no longer need her at all.'

'Will you start seeing patients again?'

'I don't know. Not the way I did before, in any case. Not in the same state of mind . . . Financially I think I can still last another three or four months . . . I'd like to have enough money to be able to spend time on a book in which all the mysteries of science would be discussed; that should humble those who claim to know everything. It would be a clear and exhaustive list of the mysteries knowledge hasn't been able to solve. In some areas, on some precise points, we get a little further ahead each day. On other points, even though they are vital, even though they affect our everyday life, we make no progress at all, and we pretend that they don't exist. Obviously I'm thinking about the selection process that takes place in the synapse and makes nervous reactions unpredictable. But I'm also thinking about the variations in the magnetic pole, which we cannot locate accurately, and which confound the illusory efforts of meteorology to control atmospheric phenomena. I'm thinking of cancer . . . There are thousands of mysteries that affect our everyday lives . . . I have no desire to return to the days of living in caves and letting lightning hit me on the head, when I know how effective a lightning rod can be in an electric storm. But I think that people like me, who practise their profession on others, should always be aware of the ignorance, and should be humble *vis-à-vis* other people, other people's problems and misery. I don't just mean psychologists and doctors, and all those who provide health care, but also those who make the laws, and the police . . . We owe it to people to show them respect, because of the mysteries within them, because of the mysteries that are beyond them, that are beyond us . . . Anyway, all that's utopian . . . I can always find work in a clinic . . . But first we have to finish the book.'

I don't know what to think any more. First that look of

hers, then her cheerfulness, and now this way she has of putting everything in order, shutting doors after opening them. Her way of organising her life all by herself. Her autonomy, her independence.

She asks, 'When are we going to get back to work?'

With that the meal is over. The waiter comes to ask if we want dessert or coffee. Before Elsa even has time to open her mouth, I say, 'No, thank you. The bill, please.'

'Do you have another engagement? You should have told me – we could have put this off until tomorrow or some other day. I'm sorry . . .'

'I don't have another engagement. Nobody's waiting for me; I have nothing to do. I'm overwhelmed, that's all.'

The waiter returns with the bill on a saucer, which he sets down next to me. Elsa puts out her hand: 'Let me pay half.'

'Absolutely not.'

'Come on, now, you'll hurt my feelings.'

'I would be the one whose feelings were hurt. Do you want people to take me for the prince consort?'

'What's come over you?'

'It's the waiter. He's annoying. You're right, let's split it . . . I haven't done a single thing right all evening.'

We settle the bill quickly, both embarrassed. Elsa leans over to pick up her handbag and begins to rise. The evening is a complete disaster.

'Listen, I must speak to you.'

'Yes? Is it about the book? Don't you want to do it any more?'

'No, that's not it. Elsa, I love you.'

I don't even look at her as I say it.

I stared at the table-cloth covered in crumbs, the plate with the money on it, my crumpled napkin . . .

'Please don't tell me that you're old enough to be my mother, that it's a question of transference . . . Don't explain about life and death and love. Don't slap me in the face . . . I love you, that's all, and I have done for a long time. I have no plans. I have no desire other than to tell you I love you. I've no intention of complicating our relationship with my feelings and constantly making a display of them. You don't have to answer, comfort me or reason with me. What's ruining my life isn't that you don't love me, because that's all right. What is ruining my life is that I haven't told you that I love you . . . I'm not big on tragedy, or even drama, despite my interest in crime novels . . . I'm a man who likes to keep out of trouble, and for the last few months I haven't been able to do that. Let me love you quietly. I want you to know that I love you and that my love, at least, is steadfast, as steadfast as the Himalayas. I'm a mountain of tenderness and affection where you can always find shelter. That's all I wanted to say. And having said it, I'm ready to go back to work with you tomorrow if you like.'

I don't even know whether she has heard the end of my tirade. When I raise my eyes to look at her, she's gone. I bound down the stairs and run down the street. No one. I've lost her. Tears well up in my eyes. At least that's positive. Because the lump that has been in my throat has been choking me. My love is gone.

No, she's in her car. I see her silhouette inside. I run, wiping my face. Perhaps I can salvage something, or at least apologise.

She sees me running towards her and gets out. We're on opposite sides of the car, with the roof between us. She's not angry; on the contrary, she's gentle. She's wearing her serious expression. We look at each other. I say: 'It's not a major problem.'

'Yes, it is.'

'No, it's simple. It's as simple as one, two, three and it's inevitable.'

'What are we going to do?'

'Well . . . We could go for a walk.'

We begin to walk down towards the Seine.

When I first moved to Paris, if ever I got lost, I always looked for the Seine. Once there, I could find my bearings again. I tell her about it. She tells me that she did the same thing.

We walk quite a way. It's mild. There are quite a few people on the pavement; passers-by separate us and we find each other again. We continue like that all the way to the Louvre. There we slow our pace. There is more room; it is darker. We descend a staircase to the quay. We go to the water's edge. We sit down, dangling our feet. We watch the river flowing by. We don't dare look at each other. Everything is in suspense, fragile. Everything could go one way or the other. We don't know.

She says: 'It seems as though we're just beginning something, but it actually started a long time ago. Perhaps we should have let it pass.'

'Abstraction, theory – that's not my strong point. I prefer to experience things . . . even sad things.'

'Well, let's start something then. Let's look at each other, at least.'

She is the mute child, the good schoolgirl, the wild woman, tenderness, all at once. She warns me gently that she is all those. My eyes tell her that I know it and that I love her. And then water blurs everything.

She says, 'What's come over us?'

After a long pause, I answer: 'I think it's what you call entropy, Elsa.'